THE WAITING PLACE

CHARL FREGONA

Editor: Victoria Canning

Publisher & design copyright holder (© 2001):
umSinsi Press
PO Box 28129
MALVERN
4055
KwaZulu Natal
South Africa
Web: http://www.umsinsi.com

Origination

Concept Design

To Marí,
with gratitude and love
for believing in me

Thanks are due to:

Felicity Keats Morrison, indefatigable creative spirit, teacher, writer and friend

Shirley Bell, my supportive and endlessly interested writing partner who kept me going

Victoria Canning whose careful, skillful editing taught me much about my writing style

Morag Erasmus for encouragement and love
Marí Peté for reading and re-reading and then demanding the next chapter, and also for the beautiful cover photography

Ester Lee for the location
The characters in this book are entirely fictitious, the events a product of the author's imagination. Any resemblance to anyone either living or dead is quite unintended and purely coincidental.

CHAPTER ONE

"Loving James. That was the sunlight of it, and the shadows. I always did love him, Anna... but, you know, it took me a long time to discern that the form of love is quite different from its conventions. You asked me to tell you a story, dearest. Hmm... a mother's wedding gift, this story... well now, let me see... just turn that way a little... I need to pin the hem. You, Anna Carney, are going to be the most beautiful bride."

That James and I were not intended for one another, and that we were not to think so, was made clear to me from a very early age. Subsequently, the events in our lives merely reinforced the idea that the McKelveys were to be treated with polite respect only, but were not to be made welcome in our home. This state of affairs had something to do with James's father, Edward McKelvey, and my mother, Johanna Whitney... Hanna.

It was different then, you know. The small conventions and social orders of our lives at

6

that time were considered to be more important than giving in to one's own feelings and desires. My mother, like all Afrikaans mothers, instilled this in me with care. We were not allowed to mention Edward or James in our home however we felt about them, but when our parents did meet face to face, as they often did at the club or at polo events in the Mount Edgecombe area, they seemed, to me, to exchange all the usual pleasantries, just as everyone else in our small society did.

"Say good afternoon to Mrs. McKelvey, Joss." Then later, on the way home, "Decisions have been made and they are to be upheld. It's not what you feel that is important, it is how others are affected." And, when I questioned that, "Yes, you must greet Mrs. McKelvey, when you see her… No, Joss, we may not have James for lunch."

My parents seemed to live like actors behind masks, carefully hiding suggestions of devastation or impropriety. No matter that whatever was between my mother and Edward McKelvey was there, unbidden, not asked for, but there, its presence underscoring the rhythm of our lives.

I admired and loved my mother more than anything... until James, that is. In that loving of her, I was exactly like my father, Kiernan Whitney. "Kicker" we called him. He seemed to love my mother with the same profound anguish that I often experienced in relation to her, and which I could not explain. She was as constant and loving towards him, as she was regarding me. But I knew of the secret distance they had between them. This distance was as profound, or more so, between my mother and the McKelveys. This I noticed particularly when they found themselves sharing a picnic basket at the polo, or Kicker and Edward found themselves in competition on the field. These significant adults seemed forever connected, forever apart.

If my mother and Edward found themselves alone - of course, like most children, I was discounted as a third party in these things and completely ignored - they seemed to want to say much. Instead they used their masks and

8

conversed in stilted, acceptable conversations. I always loved her most of all then.

I wanted to know what bond they held between them - my graceful, well brought up mother and Edward Whitney, dark and powerful, a sugar baron of a man - but I learned very quickly myself to mask my conversations regarding the McKelveys in exactly the same careful way as my mother. It made my father extremely angry if I mentioned them in his presence but their absence. It was such a mystery.

Even James could not explain these things to me. If I asked him about his father, he would just look at me puzzled and say, "Come on, Titch. Get that saddle sorted out. What do I know about these things, man." Then we would leap onto the horses and go flying across the cane field gullies and the thunder of the horses' hooves with the smell of the black soil flying up in our faces became the most important, most exhilarating focus for my wondering.

No matter what anyone said, I knew it was

why my mother had such shadows in her face… shadows that only those who loved her deeply could see. These shadows formed the dark passages in the concerto she and I were to share all these years in a sort of counterpoint to the McKelveys. I therefore determined that I would live unconventionally, and do and say exactly what I felt. I was not going to be like my mother.

This was easier said than done.

I could ride better than anyone in the district, even James, though he was older by ten years. However, I felt he made up for this because he never ever discounted my presence like the others. He had plenty of time to show me where the mongoose had crushed the hen's eggs in an orgy of greed below the yellowed Oregon floorboards of our house. Certainly, he taught me all I knew about river birds, and the fish eagles hovering high above them sweeping in from the sea with their wild haunted calling. We lay for hours watching the birds wheeling above us in search of the mysterious dappled fish in the shadowed rivers running below our sprawling lawn edges.

"Look here, Titch," he'd say, and coax a miniature tree frog onto my hand, a perfect ornament of quivering grace and beautiful music box sounds. "It's called hyperolius." Breathless with wonder, I would hold its tiny body and look at James with shining eyes.

"You know everything, James," I would say. He would just tousle my hair and laugh.

"Not everything, Titch. Not everything. There's a deal to go before that."

Then James turned nineteen and went to university in the Cape. I did not see him again for a full decade, although in the beginning I wrote him many anxious letters so that he would know the mongoose babies were thriving and one had killed a snake while I was watching.

He never wrote back.

"Why are you crying so, Joss?" my mother asked and I could not tell her because I knew shadows would begin to lengthen at home and that she would feel them. If I told her, I knew she would draw back to the veranda and sit in the sinking light of the sun, sipping tea from a thin china cup with fluted silvered edges. And only I could hear her sighing. My mother was filled with mystery.

I loved her with all the passion of my small being at these times. Her hands held the fragrance of honeysuckle and when she breathed it seemed that the earth had settled into a familiar place in the vast universe. In soft half-lit mornings, I would slip from my tangled bed, long before the sun began to touch the mosquito netting on my windows, and walk down the veranda to stand outside her long narrow doors until I heard her say, "Come on in, Joss. Come in, darling." I would clamber into the huge double bed beside her, her warm velvet body against mine, as I settled into her arms.

Next to her, the mattress still held an impression of my father, by now long gone from the stables for a quota of hard work on the Heritage estates. He always left well before the breakfast gongs were beaten. I would run my hands along the dents left by his large body in the mattress and feel the lingering warmth beside us. Lying there beside my mother in the colouring light thrown out by a bronze sky, I would lie wide-eyed and expectant for what the new day would be bringing to my safe and beautiful world.

CHAPTER TWO

The worst thing after James left, were the interminably dragging terms at boarding school. I cried profusely every time my mother or father or both drove me back to Maritzburg. It was not that I missed my parents while I was away. I saw them often enough. They enjoyed driving up to watch me ride competitively and were often there as members of the school's governing body. My crying had more to do with the curtailment of the freedom I enjoyed at home amongst the wide, waving cane of my father's plantations.

My father owned the original Heritage estates, including most of Mount Edgecombe, and several thousand acres besides. At home, I could range across the fields riding for hours on end and watching the great clouds banking up in the immense vault of the sky without having to account to anyone. The harsh cries of the hadedahs caught my imagination as they flitted above in hooked cursives, and I could never the hear the soaring haunting calls of the fish eagles without my emotions flying as high as their own wheeling, soaring rapture. In the wind, lay the fragrance of Joss sticks and masala and everywhere Indian women moved across landscaped terraces of cane and black soil, bringing tea and puri phuta for the men in the fields.

Now and then a Hindu wedding party would pass my way, exotic glittering finery offset by the deep rich bougainvillaea-coloured materials of saris and punjabis. As they passed atop a rickety cart drawn by two white oxen, their bangles and headdresses sequinned a reflection of their joy and excitement into the sun. The bride and groom were so beautiful with their dark liquid eyes and their thin, fine bodies. I would rein in while they passed, listening to the banging of the drums, my mind garbed in their garlands of bright flowers.

One day I rode far enough across the fields to stumble across something that began to reveal some of the masks my parents wore with each other. At the edge of the plantations, lay an ancient and wonderfully ornate Hindu temple, no longer used. I was anxious to investigate its carved walls, which I had never seen, so I dismounted and tied Vagabond to a log at the edge of the clearing from which the sun-washed, mossy temple walls rose.

As I crouched to examine the writhing bas-relief figures on the crumbling walls, it became clear to me that they were celebrating the same rituals as the horses and my dogs in the yards and the paddocks at home. Taken aback, I withdrew into the dense green bush along the temple walls. As I did so, a lithe sari-clad figure darted into the bright sunlight in front of the temple. She hesitated looking eagerly forward, and began to unwind the intricate yards of cloth draped around her body. The silvery crimson sari folds settled into the dust at her feet. She wore a short choli shot through with threads of silver. It barely covered her midriff. Her upper lip was beaded with moisture.

I froze with expectation and sure enough a

young man of about her age moved into the clearing and reached for her hand. When I saw the look that passed between them, I began to apprehend something of what happened, and was still happening perhaps, between my mother and Edward Whitney. I knew I should leave and walked quickly to untie Vagabond's reins. As I threw my leg across his back and settled into the saddle, I heard the girl moan. I looked across my shoulder at them. He had unhooked the small buttons of her jacket and was pulling back the damp cloth from her breasts.

I drove my heels into Vagabond's sides and we thundered away. I dared not look back a second time. Vagabond had picked up my restiveness and powered out of the bush across a firebreak in the cane. I urged him on recklessly, fiercely glad to be caught up in having to control him so that I would not lose my balance and die in the flying of his hooves.

My days at boarding school were, by contrast to the free life at home, a matter of restriction and study. Looking back after all these years I must say I admire the fortitude of my teachers although, of course, I did not appreciate the fact then. The arrival of Kerry D'Unienville, my second cousin, did much to ease the endless chafing I felt there. You could see that we had sprung from the same dark Irish stock. Siobhan was much smaller than me, more fine-boned. The main thing was she shared my wild enthusiasm for riding and it was a relief to have someone sensible to talk to. The other girls in the dormitory had one thing on their minds – and that was certainly neither point-to-point or horse-feed.

Kerry proved a sympathetic and interested listener. I shared my devastating loss regarding James with her during the long drawn-out hours after school, as the shadows lengthened and the harsh sun gathered in a soft purple ambience from flowering jacarandas in the school grounds. She was very interested in James and admired my framed photo of him enviously since he was already a grown man. We agreed that the boys at the neighbouring school were little more than children — despite, by the way, the scornful views we had of our dormitory colleague's interests and concerns.

In return, Kerry told me about her fears for her mother, Milly, my father's cousin. Privately, I thought that she was a seriously silly woman, but Kerry and I became the best and closest of friends and she always did stand by me for the rest of her life, so I never mentioned what I felt in this regard.

"You know, Joss, I wish my mother was more like yours," I remember her saying. (This was a constant refrain in our rambling, conversations that took place endlessly despite the piles of blue-lined homework books forgotten beneath our elbows.) "I can't remember my dad, you know. I wonder if he was anything like yours," Kerry would continue. Then, after a pause, "I bet she is going to marry Uncle Beau." At this, I remember giving an arch to my inner eyebrow, but continued looking at her steadily. Uncle Beau was another of our distantly shared relatives. He was a total embarrassment to everyone in the family... Kerry's mother, obviously, saw something in him. "Imagine that, Joss, being the bridesmaid at your own mother's wedding. How embarrassing."

She would pull a face, and I would assure her that her mother would not be ridiculous enough to go so far. "Stoop so low" were the words that sprang to my mind. The man smelled of lavender pomade and silver brushes. He *drank*. No one could take him seriously. I changed the subject.

"Did you see that guy running in the cross country yesterday, Ker?" She gazed at me quizzically.

"Which one, Joss?" Suddenly I felt shy. I had just been going on about James again and I didn't want Kerry to think I was flighty after my recent thoughts regarding her mother.

"Was it that blond one that you were talking to for so long?" she asked innocently. I coloured. "Oh, it's serious," she continued, laughing. "I thought he seemed rather keen on you, Jossie. Are you going to the matric dance with him, then?"

20

"I'll think about it, Ker. Who's taking you?" In fact I had already said yes to Peter Carney, a Michael Hall sportsman, and was looking forward to this new phase in my experience with great excitement.

"Robert, although he hasn't asked yet," said Kerry with her mouth turned down. "You'll always get the tall, blond and handsome ones, Cuz. The likes of us will end up with the Roberts of the world." I protested feebly.

How wrong Kerry proved to be about that!

Whenever I think back on that final dance at school, I remember how Peter shone... filled with excitement and pride, handsome and tall and young. What a night that was...I remember now I had to hold his wrist to keep his hand from moving up under the chiffon sheath I wore, and he kissed me with whisky on his breath. Oh, I remember how dark the sky was and the stars falling from heaven like rain on the night of my first kiss.

Ten years is a long time. I was glad when

school was over. Wykeford, in my mother's opinion, had been good for me. If the truth were told, my matric year at boarding school had been filled with the excitement of getting Peter Carney to take me seriously. As far as I was concerned, Peter had everything going for him. He was tall and angular, the best sportsman, and I really was keen on the insistent way he started kissing me at every opportunity after the matric dance. I began to feel he was going to make a fine husband... such was my wisdom at nineteen.

Looking back, the flood of pictures in my mind concerns him mostly. As I think back along the stern of my memories, I can see his hands on the steering wheel, confident and strong.

It feels fine, then, to be sitting next to him in my white ball gown pressed into the fragrant new leather of his car. I see him smiling and I am touching the back of his head with the back of my hand. I feel his hand on my thigh and excitement and pleasure that I could make him want to do that.

"Well, how does it feel to be on your way to the ball?"

"You've been drinking, Pete," I say.

"Yes, I have. And your Dad didn't help the situation either."

"Don't let Kicker worry you, Pete," I am saying.

"No... but he is your dad, you know." This makes me laugh.

"Yes, he is at that," I say in answer and tousle his hair so that he can cool off and concentrate on the road ahead...

Let's see how the dress looks now, Anna... Step back from the mirror so you can see the train. That looks just fine, doesn't it?

CHAPTER THREE

Peter had arrived early that evening to be introduced to my parents, and we were on our way to the Sugar Ball held each year at the country club. My father and Peter had made a fine pair in their dinner jackets, standing before the Burmese teak bar running the full length of the lounge, Peter carefully imitating my dad in manliness and heartiness. Peter had rather nervously accepted several generous tots of whisky, decanted from a cut glass bottle by my father, and had been drinking too much and too quickly.

When he pulled in to the club parking lot, he opened the door of the car for me and, seeing that he was unsteady, I entered the foyer with him arm in arm. Peter was laughing and I was too, caught up in his mood. As I looked up from our clowning, I caught the gaze of a man who had just turned from the reception counter towards us. He was looking at me inquiringly, as if he wanted to say something. For a moment it seemed somehow I knew him, but Peter swept me up the short flight of carpeted stairs and we entered the ballroom.

My mother and Kicker had already arrived and were sitting at a table consisting of Kerry, her mother and Uncle Beau. Millicent D'Unienville immediately began to gesticulate wildly, indicating that we should join the party at once.

"My dear," she screeched. "Have you heard? James McKelvey is back from the States. Apparently he will be here tonight! Aren't you pleased, Joss?" Peter stiffened and Kerry looked up at me appealingly. "Weren't you and James an item, Jossie? Didn't you once have a crush on him?" Milly continued loudly and gaily, with the determined air of a matchmaker. Kicker had turned red of face at the mention of the McKelvey name and my mother had moved in her chair slightly, as if to settle herself.

There was always that same reaction at the mention of the McKelvey name.

"Oh, Auntie Milly, really. I was ten years old. He must be antediluvian by now..." I said firmly.

"Not that ancient. Just a little older, more solid, perhaps," a well-remembered voice, sounding wry, sounding deeper and older, interrupted me. There was a moment of confused silence, during which I managed to avoid gasping. So, it had been James at the reception counter looking so quizzically at me.

"Hello, James. Welcome back." My mother was restoring social order in her graceful, understated way, giving me time to recover from my faux pas and compose myself before I turned to take the outstretched hand of James McKelvey.

"James. You didn't write," I said inappropriately.

"Write?" he asked curiously. "Was I supposed to?"

I laughed and said, "Sorry. I mean, hello, how are you, James?" I was pleased that my mother's training came to the fore and my own masks came down so easily. I was conscious only that I should smile coolly as his deep eyes, his wonderful dark eyes, gazed warmly into my own. I withdrew the hand he was still holding.

"May I introduce you to Peter Carney, James?"

"Ah, pleased to meet you, Peter. By God, Titch, you've grown into a beautiful woman." I thought my heart was about to vault from my body with joy and confusion.

"Thank you. Do you know everyone, James? Millicent and Kerry D'Unienville. Uncle Beau Whitney," I said in the coolest of Wykeford tones.

"What did they teach you about sugar at that fancy college of yours, James? Anything?" my father grunted and they shook hands briefly.

"Plenny to know 'bout shugah, eh, James. Have a whisky, old cock," managed Uncle Beau becoming aware against a backdrop of Aunt Milly's genteel cries that he needed to make a social contribution. "Here, James, me'old slush, one f'r the road, eh? Hev 'nother, what," Beau enunciated carefully, waving his glass, and peering intently into Peter's eyes.

"That's Peter, Beau. Here's James, Beau. This side, Beau," Auntie Milly said firmly, pointing him in the right direction.

"Oh, shorry, old cock. Thought you were James f'r moment there, laddie. Thenk ye, m'dear, thenk ye.' Bliged. Very 'bliged. Hev a drink, James, old boy." He subsided onto Milly's anxiously awaiting arm, smiling benevolently. Auntie Milly patted him soothingly.

When all the niceties were done, my mother offered James a place at the table, which he accepted in an open, glad fashion. He appeared to converse easily with my father though my father gave him more than his usual gruff and blunt run for his conversational money. James spent some time talking to Peter about rugby, too. Watching him, I saw that he had filled out and there was a pattern of fine lines in his tanned, well-shaven face. There was nothing boyish in him, none of the slightly hesitant deference I remembered when he was nineteen. Now, as he chatted to my mother and Kerry, I saw that

James had returned, self assured, successful, suave, very much at home in the company of men like my father.

It was, I remember, a humid Durban night, when only languidly stirring ceiling fans provided any form of relief. The club ballroom had a wonderful view of the sea from immense windows overlooking the greenest golf course in Natal although, by now, the sea had receded into a silky and indigo night. A string of ships festooned the horizon with a necklace of illumination. Chandeliers dangling from the pressed metal ceilings dazzled with their own splendour, reflecting patterns on glass panes that were shot through with images of couples dancing in front of the bandstand. Standing outside on the broad balcony, looking in, I could see my mother and Kicker dancing. They were holding each other close. I could see that Kicker was happy.

Peter returned with another glass in his hand. He was beginning to sound like Uncle Beau. He put his arm around me.

"Sorry, Josh. Had a bit too much whishky."

He was weaving and by now definitely needed my support to keep upright.

"Oh, Peter. Don't have any more." He took a sip.

"Jus' a bit. Jus' a li'l bit. Come here, sweetness. Lemme give you a kiss." For the very first time in my life I felt the instinctive withdrawal that I had so often wondered about when I had discerned it in my mother.

"Come on, Pete. We'd better get you home." He flung his arms around my neck, and got violently ill, throwing up his food and drink on me. I felt dreadfully angry, and sorry, for Peter. I knew my reaction to James earlier in the evening had given his confidence a real kick. He pulled his black jacket off and began to try and wipe off the worst of the mess.

"Oh Peter, really. Come on, let's go home," I said miserably.

"Good idea. Let's get this young man out of here and into bed." To my absolute mortification, I found James standing beside me.

He matter of factly took charge of Peter,

while I repaired to the ladies to clean up the worst of the damage, my face aflame.

"Let's take him home to Heritage... in his car, Joss... You can drive me back here when you've changed." Neither James nor I spoke on the way back. Peter lay on the back seat groaning and singing wildly, reeking of drink and sickness.

"Have a shower, Titch. I'll wait in the lounge," said James, picking up a cigar from a silver box. I was embarrassed and reluctant to do so but returned resolutely to the lounge after I had finished in the shower. James stood up as I entered.

"Well now, that's how I remember you," he said appreciatively. I had pulled on a pair of riding denims and a cotton blouse. I smiled wryly.

"James, I'm really sorry about all this." He dismissed my apology.

"I've been there once or twice, Titch. I was young once." He smiled again, seeing his gentle irony had found its mark.

"James, when you're nine, someone who's

nineteen seems manifestly old."

He opened the door for me. He laughed. "That's my girl. That's the girl I remember." He paused and looked down at his feet. "Look, there's a miniature frog hopping along all by himself here on the veranda. Look, Joss, isn't he the most perfect thing?" We were surrounded by its music-box noises. He crouched to have a closer look. I felt nine again and in the dizzy vaulting moment, crouched beside him on the veranda, I felt was going to say, "You know everything, James." And that James would touch my hair before he replied, "Not everything, Titch. Not everything. There's a deal to go before that."

CHAPTER FOUR

Well, Anna, to get back to the business of masks. I only ever heard my parents raise their voices to each other once. It seemed to tear apart the curtain of our lives, allowing me, at nineteen, to glimpse some of the darker scenes maturity brings. It was such a shocking thing, to hear my mother raise her voice to Kicker, and although generally Kicker made no bones about making his feelings plain, I had never heard him shout at my mother before. He was a difficult man, but, nevertheless, I used to think that my mother understood him better than anyone and that she gentled him.

Kicker held no truck with fools. When his will was crossed, he displayed an Irish vocabulary and a half, and very loud it was too. But even in his most violent rages, Kicker responded to my mother's lift of an eyebrow and her "Kicker, that will do," in a quiet tone of regret. Then my father would take hold on himself, and put his hand to her chin, kissing her in his strong hearty fashion.

And, as always, I was aware of the slightest sense of withdrawal in her, disciplined, to be sure, by years of adherence and submission to the complexity of this. Oh, I loved him too, when she drew his arm through his as a reward for his control, and urged him to inspect the new roses she had put in, or to mourn with her the destruction the monkeys had caused in the fruit trees. Not until much later did I begin to see what it was that had made him do the things he did

The events that led to their argument that evening had their root James McKelvey's return. James had called several times after the night of the Sugar Ball. He was received courteously by my parents, and enthusiastically by me. I soon found that he seemed to enjoy talking about our early days and I got along with him as easily as ever. Despite the intervening years, he seemed to have retained some of the sense of wonder he had felt in the days of the mongooses, and had passed on to me when we were out there on the lands amongst the wild calls of fish eagles and the wheeling of the hadedahs. I phoned him as often as I could find an excuse to do so after his return.

I was filled with pleasure at discovering that he still loved riding. We spent hours ranging across the fields, leaving Peter at the house waiting for us. Peter always seemed glad to see us back, and had as much to say to James as I did. But it was always about cricket or rugby. Sometimes I wished Peter could share the feelings that I had being out there in the heart of those rolling, verdant hills... somehow my passion for riding seemed to exclude him, that he excluded me with his endless sports talk. I did not feel this way with James. I knew James was a busy and hardworking man and that his friends and business associates seemed very knowledgeable and sophisticated, at ease with life, but he always seemed to have time for me.

One evening, James and I came galloping

through the lower section of the plantations on one of these rides. As we rounded the bend in the gravel, we almost collided with Kicker, astride his own roan on some hurried mission. An expletive filled the air as his horse danced wildly, surprised by our appearance, fighting the severe control Kicker was forced to exercise to keep him from bolting.

"Bugger it, Joss. What the hell are you doing thundering around the corner in that stupid way... and, McKelvey, you should know better. That horse of yours is just about blown." Kicker had his hands full with his startled roan.

"Sorry," muttered James. "I surely could have prevented surprising you, sir." Our own horses were rolling their eyes, high stepping and fighting their bits.

"You better get home, Joss. It's late. Your mother will be waiting for you. What are you doing riding around the countryside in this bloody ridiculous fashion, anyway?" Kicker continued irritably. I dug my heels into Vagabond and pulled away, surprised that

James did not follow immediately. I was annoyed and rode hard to get away from them both.

I was rubbing Vagabond down in his stable, securing him for the night with a large helping of feed, when James arrived. His face was clouded in a way I had never seen before. I was incensed with Kicker. They had obviously had words that James, certainly, had not appreciated.

"I'm sorry, James. I shouldn't have been chasing so madly. It could have gone badly if Kicker had been unseated. He's getting on, you know... he always has been crotchety... it's nothing new."

James seemed to collect himself. "Never you mind, Titch. It was a fine ride, young lady, but I probably deserved a reprimand." James's voice had a hard edge to it. I had not heard it before. He put his hand on my shoulder, seeming to look at me in a new way, his eyes searching my face carefully. "You're not to worry, Titch. It's fine." He spoke gently. Suddenly I was aware of an altered tension between us. I could feel the warm rush of his breath on my face. I wanted to put my mouth against his. I knew I was going to.

"Keep your hand there, James," I said. "It feels fine there." It was the moment of change. Nothing would ever detract from the ecstasy of it, of his other hand coming up to my waist, of a completed waiting that gathered my soul up into it.

Save that his face tightened and his body stiffened. "No, Joss. I don't think so… I don't think so," he said, moving his hand from my shoulder, and bringing up his other hand to clasp my trembling fingers.

"McKelvey! Get out of here! Get away from her, you whelp! I'll thrash you witless, you upstart!" Kicker strode into the front of the stable. He rounded on James in a towering, screaming rage, and brought down his raised fist, cutting James across the shoulder with his riding crop. James scarcely flinched and left off his holding of my hands, turning to face Kicker.

"You've said your say, Whitney," he said.

"And I had mine." I could see he was angrier than Kicker had ever been. His face was suffused with a more terrible rage than I had ever seen, even in my father. "Joss is safe from me, Whitney!" he spat out. "Put that bloody thing away, man." Snorting with contempt, James wrenched Kicker's crop from him and threw it to the ground, and, turning on his heel, stalked away.

I felt the tearing of the heart that signals the end of childhood. Such is the dying of innocent belief. I could not stop the tears running down my face. "You should not do that, Dad." Kicker turned to me as if coming out of a deep sleep. "You should not do that to the people you love, Dad." He seemed momentarily confused. He realised, then, that I was fighting to control my own anguished horror and a look of lacerated confusion passed over his face, which brought my own anger under immediate control. He seemed like a snared animal, struggling to stay perfectly still against the larger pain of pulling against a wire digging deeper into its throat.

"Oh, yes, you must... yes, you do, Jossie. That's the way of it. One does it, one crucifies those you love most," he said, his voice cracking like broken glass. I could not bear it. I put my face against Vagabond's side and wept without restraint. Kicker hesitated. Then, clearing his throat, he walked away into the shadows.

It was a long time before I could go up to join my parents. Late that night, I heard my mother knocking at my door. I pulled the hook from its brass hoop and turned the key to let her in. From behind her, the sounds of the night rushed in. Painted tree frogs were cheeping from the towering fig tree on the edge of the veranda and I could hear the rustle of its huge copper leaves tumbling about on the lawn in the wind.

"Mama," I begged. "Mama, what is it with James? What is it?" She held me while I cried, but remained perfectly still. Later, I realised that she had cried, too... that, in fact, she had said, "Jossie, I'm so sorry. I'm so sorry." I realise, now, that I was too distraught, and too young, to consider anything but my own emotions. I did not know that she was asking my forgiveness in the silence of her crying.

Yes, I do remember my mother sitting at her customary place late next afternoon. She was surrounded by billowing lace, as the wind flicked the curtains backwards and forwards through the long narrow French doors along the length of the veranda. A storm was building up along the horizon piling huge banks of cloud into the sunset. The air, sketching swirls and eddies, plucked wisps of soot in from the burning cane fields and scattered them on the lace around us, and all the while the shuttered doors rattled on their hinges.

My mother did not see me lying there amongst the profusion of leaves cast down in the mounting wind by the fig. I knew she was waiting for Kicker. He had been out all day controlling the firing of the fields and she was anxious for him. It was the dangerous, arduous time for the cane planters, the burning of the cane. Kicker had not counted on the wind coming up. However, I knew, also, that the storm behind the wind would take care of any runaway fires that might threaten to destroy his carefully managed work. This night, because of the rising storm, my father would be safe from the routine danger of being burnt alive in his own cane fields.

After a hard, bitter night and a long day of sad speculation, I had come to the conclusion that I was being silly about James. He was so much older than me. I was putting him under the pressure of an immature infatuation, experienced long ago as a small girl, and built into something he was not part of. I felt embarrassed that I had tried to get him to kiss me and resolved to apologise for exposing him to Kicker's wrath, not once, but twice, on the same evening. I had begun to feel better and savoured being out there on the lawn, with the bitter-sweet smell of burnt sugar and the sun bursting into bronze and incense about me.

I was further calmed by the fact that my mother was waiting for my father on the veranda at her usual place. This she had done on each of the days since she had married him. Next to her on the low cane table stood a silver tray. The silver soda siphon and cut glass decanter of gin sparkled in the pools of blurred light spilling from the doorways. I heard, as she did, the commotion of the grooms as he arrived and the solid crunch of leaves as he strode up from the stables from the edge of the front lawns, and entered his home by the sweep of steps at the front of the veranda. The maid received his jacket and crop and scurried away to initiate preparations for his dinner. As always, he bent to kiss my mother and then settled into the wicker chair next to hers to share with her the events of the day.

After a while he said to her, "You're unusually quiet tonight, my dear." She must have nodded. I was no longer able to see them clearly from where I lay in the rapidly gathering dusk.

"Kiernan," I heard her say, tentatively. "Tonight we'll have to discuss James McKelvey. Joss is very upset, darling." There was an ominous silence. I heard him spit out an oath. "Kiernan…"

"There will be no mention of the McKelvey name in my house, Johanna," he interrupted, his voice rising.

"Kiernan… she's in love with the boy." There was the sound of a thud and a staccato of breaking glass. He must have flung the gin decanter in his hand at the veranda wall. I jerked upright. I could just make out that they had both stood up and were facing each other. "That nothing to do with us," my mother shouted. I was stunned to hear her raising her voice and stood up myself, transfixed, terrified. "You cannot punish Jossie for me, Kiernan. You can't make her pay for me. Let them be! Let them be, Kiernan! Let her love who she will," my mother continued hysterically. My father's next words were like physical blows to me.

"I'll not have another McKelvey whore in my house, Johanna. That bastard's been at her since the day he got back!" I heard my mother gasp and another sound, as if someone had been slapped. Whatever it was, it seemed to bring Kicker's building tirade to a dead halt. I heard my mother's voice, still raised, trembling. " I'm not afraid of you, Kiernan. I'm not afraid of you! But I am frightened of the way you can destroy those that love you. I'm afraid of the way you can destroy yourself."

"Johanna... Jossie... Ah, Joss, " Kicker said bitterly in the darkness. "You promised. You said that you would never again say his name. You said so, Jossie."

"I did not say his name, Kicker. It was not his name, I said." In my mother's now lowered quieter voice lay the years of her anguish, all the years of her guilt.

In that vaulting black horrible moment I had fallen into, I sought precariously for a meaning, desperate for an escape from implications, inferences I could not bear to sustain. A picture of my mother wrapped in Edward McKelvey's arms etched itself into my soul. Masks began to make sense and, for the first time, I reached for one. I put it on firmly and began then the long process of hiding my feelings about James from myself.

After a while it got easy to blame him for being the cause of my disillusionment and, therefore, not to call and explain, and later, not to love him any more the way I had always done.

CHAPTER FIVE

Peter Carney and I did not get married immediately. There were the varsity years and then the announcements to respective parents that we would be travelling together overseas for a year or two. I must say Kicker took it well. He seemed to think Peter would look after me admirably and joked about not bringing any surprises home. My mother asked me later, as I was packing, if I felt I was doing the right thing. I hugged her but between us was a feeling that she had no right to ask me such a question.

And so Peter and I got to know each other on the streets of London, in the back lanes of France, on the beaches of Greece... the last days of our youth squandered in the back of a van and sometimes, just sometimes, in a flood of passion and joy. Somewhere in all of that, we resumed our responsibilities and returned home, cured of the restless, shiftlessness thrust upon all my generation by the advent of the seventies and the certain knowledge of things coming in on the wind of the future.

When, at last, I returned to my home in Mount Edgecombe, I was shocked to see how Kicker, always hearty and bluff, had aged. On the other hand, my mother was as lovely as ever. The decade in age that separated them was beginning to show. I noticed that all my postcards had been carefully pinned to a board in her study, my letters carefully stored in a walnut case on her dresser.

It was seemed so fine to be back where I belonged.

Both my parents were excited and pleased when Peter, rather traditionally, asked my father for my hand in the smoking room the night after we got back. Kicker and Peter celebrated with full honours and were heard roaring my father's favourite drinking songs into the small hours. My mother asked me, "Do you love him, Joss?" and I nodded reassuringly in my sophisticated Wykeford way. I could see she was relishing the idea of an immense social occasion. She would have the Mount Edgecombe bridge and tea party community occupied for a number of years in deep admiration and endless pleasure at recalling some aspect or the other of *the* wedding.

Peter and I had also been up to his parents' farm in the Peacevale valley for the night. This was where Peter was to begin working after our marriage. His father, Tim, had already initiated plans for the building of our home in the folds of the road near their old farmhouse, a beautiful old whitewashed abode covered in crimson bougainvillaea and he wanted to discuss the plans with us. To begin with, I was touched by the welcome Peter's people gave me. I had met his parents only briefly before we went overseas. They seemed excited and eager about our wedding and promised to drive to Mount Edgecombe early on the day of our engagement.

A pleasant afternoon of homemade scones and Earl Grey tea, which I hate, served under a tea cosy under a manicured patio was marred only slightly by Ella Carney's rather pursed comment that I had waited so long before getting round to marrying her son. By which I understood her to mean that she did not approve of the fact that Peter and I shared a bedroom. Other pointed remarks followed in ensuing silences. She had not seen nor heard from her son for years and wasn't that too bad of Peter, she said, looking directly at me. However, wasn't it nice that Peter was marrying into a family with some standing. Some of the pleasure at meeting them began to dissipate.

I was surprised to hear her utter her observations in a slightly exaggerated BBC accent because old Tim, Peter's father, spoke in broad and unaffected Lancashire tones, even after his forty years in South Africa. "Eh, lass. Have another cuppa then afore we shut t'kettle. Orr some soider. We got some English soider, streight from the hills of Lancashire, like, if you would take't i'stead," he said comfortably. The cider tasted so much better than the tea, though Ella continued to sip rather crossly at her teacup and then poured another cup of tea for herself with some emphasis after the old man ignored her suggestions and placed a couple of cider glasses in front of us with oblivious bonhomie.

I also met Peter's elegant blonde sister, Iris, for the first time and found I liked her rather well too, even if she did speak much of "home", meaning England, and "last outposts", meaning Natal. She was quite glamorous and awfully elegant. Ella seemed to have passed a kind of embarrassment about origins on to her daughter, and I wished that it had not been so. Nevertheless, I began to look forward to my new life as a farmer's wife, tucked away in the craggy valley skirted by the towering drama of Key Ridge, which rose from behind it. On closer acquaintance, they seemed nice enough, despite a few idiosyncrasies. Every family had its Uncle Beau I guessed.

Distressed to hear that my old mount, Vagabond, had been put down while I was away, I accompanied Kicker just a few weeks before my engagement party to try out a mare one of the neighbours was selling. She was a beautiful chestnut with a broad chest and a fine step, and I asked for her to be delivered next day. I was keen to visit my old wild haunts as soon as possible and see what changes there had been.

While we were driving home, Kicker told me the plantations were doing as well as ever, regardless of the problems caused by the large company take-overs that had been happening recently. I did not press the point as Peter had already told me that James McKelvey was heading up one of its divisions and that Edward, his father, was on the company board as chairman. In fact, Peter and I had seen Sarah McKelvey that very morning in Umhlanga, where we had had my engagement ring fitted. She had nodded in her usual distant way from under the broad sweep of her fashionable hat when, after some effort, she recognised me.

I was up before dawn to saddle the new mare, the very day after she arrived. It had been a long time since I sat astride a horse but, as she broke into a canter and I heard the familiar creaking of the leather and the clinking bit, a familiar peace edged into me. The early light flashed in and out of the trees in spilled profusion as I left the plantation and rode into the deeper bush. It was so fine to be out there in the fragile, delicate air just before the oppressing humidity came rolling in from the sea. I let the mare have her head. After a while, I became aware that my thigh muscles were trembling. I had lost the tone I needed to ride for a long gallop, the result of so many non-riding years, so I pulled her up. Above me fish eagles called and I waited entranced before dismounting to allow my legs a period of recovery. It was a mistake. I could not summon the strength to pull myself back into the saddle and, in the ridiculous position of hanging helplessly at half-mast onto stirrup leathers while my mare stepped nervously backwards and forwards, I met James McKelvey again.

"Well, Joss," he said, "looks like you've gone soft on that long journey of yours?" I laughed. There was nothing to do but drop off and tie my mare to a branch and shake the hand James proffered, before sinking gratefully on to a flat rock, while James found a suitable place to tie his own mount.

"I'm afraid so, James," I answered ruefully. "It's been a long time since I've had a ride… And a long time since I saw you last." He sat on the rock beside me. The sunlight flickered through the movement of leaves.

"Yes, it has, Titch, I must say." He was quite unconscious of the fact that he had called me by the childish nickname he had once given me. "Three, nearly four, years if I'm not mistaken," he continued. "And that? Who's the lucky fellow, Joss? Who got to put that ring on your finger?"

"Oh, Peter. Peter Carney. You remember him, don't you? We're celebrating our engagement on Saturday… What about coming, James?" James looked at me doubtfully. He was older than I remembered; his hair flecked with grey.

"Oh, don't worry about Kicker, James. Age has mellowed him. He's not likely to worry about our family feud, now." It was James's turn to laugh.

"Him? Mellow? Granite doesn't mellow. It doesn't even wear. Nevertheless, I'd love to be there. Just to see if he has."

After chatting pleasantly for a while, James helped me mount, cupping his hands for me to place my boot so I could hoist myself up. As I pressed my hand against the hard muscle of his shoulder and pushed upwards, my heart vaulted in my body, and I slipped with the unexpectedness of it, falling against the horse.

"Steady. Steady," said James, catching me in his arms as the mare jumped forward. I wanted all of time to hold still while I sorted out the conflict I'd plummeted into, but he merely swung me up into the saddle, and we rode our separate ways. I found myself thinking about him while I rode home in the gathering heat. I found myself speculating about the ridges of his muscles, and wondering if he ever thought about me.

CHAPTER SIX

Though it was so long ago, nearly twenty-five years now, I remember clearly that the enjoyment I felt at being back in Mount Edgecombe continued on to the night of the engagement party. The party was held, like all significant occasions at the Country Club, that wonderful old Durban building once the offices and stables of the officers of the Natal Mounted Rifles. I enjoyed a new intimacy with my mother at that time, shopping for something more suitable to wear in the many pretentiously exclusive little Umhlanga designer boutiques. She seemed a little startled at my new interest in fashion and style, and remarked once or twice, in rather a surprised way, that I had developed expensive tastes on my travels.

I was looking forward to seeing my old friends, especially Kerry D'Unienville, with whom I had maintained a regular correspondence while in Europe. And, of course, I was covertly looking forward to seeing James. My mother looked startled when I mentioned that I had invited James to the party. However, I dismissed her characteristic eyebrow lift with a hurried, "Oh, Mother, he would do for Kerry. We can't have her sitting next to Uncle Beau and Auntie Milly the whole evening. Dad will just have to contain himself." She continued to look doubtful, but persuaded perhaps by my new acquiescence in everything else, she made out an invitation to him.

When Pete and I arrived at the club for our engagement, I remembered the night of our matric dance, that earlier dance emerging now from this blurred pattern of memories flowing through my mind. He was proud, excited, shining, and achingly handsome in his tuxedo. As usual, he had had a few before we left, although that slightly heady odour of whisky and aftershave was so much part of him now, I hardly noticed it. Peter was fun. I knew that the night ahead would hold more than a party for both of us and the thought was, in itself, intoxicating.

We found James McKelvey standing at the reception counter. On this occasion however, he recognised us immediately and congratulated Peter heartily. In this way, the three of us entered the ballroom together and caused a slight stir. We talked to James a little longer, and then, noticing Kerry and her mother in the corner sitting next to my reprobate old uncle, asked James if he would mind rescuing her for the evening.

Auntie Milly outdid herself that evening, both in dress and conversation. She wore a glittering blue dress bedecked with a bodice of black tassels, her hair draped in sequined net. I could see she was intent on completely dazzling Uncle Beau who sat propped up in the chair beside her, snorting occasionally and blinking in a rather confused way. Kerry and I greeted each other with glad cries and I put forward my suggestion that James join her table. I could not help noticing how eagerly she accepted the invitation.

Auntie Milly greeted us effusively.

"Oh, my dears. How wonderful to see you young lovebirds back! All ready to trip down the aisle of matrimony, you lucky young things. How wonderful! Don't you think it's too wonderful, Beaumont?" Uncle Beau roused himself momentarily.

"Oh, eh, what? W'nf'l, indeed. Yesh, w'nf'l, m'dear. Ah, Joss, how's m'gel?" He paused beaming benignly and, noticing James, continued, "You an' James getting hished, I hear. Very good. Fine filly, Jossie, James. Rides like a jockey, what! V'ry good James, old cock, v'ry good. Couldn't hev chosen better."

"Oh Beau, honestly. It's Peter. *Peter* and Jossie are getting married, my dear," Aunt Milly screeched gently at him, patting him consolingly, pointing him, once more, in the right direction.

"Oh? Eh? Peter? Shorry. Much 'bliged, Milly m'dear, much 'bliged… Peter. Yes, Peter. Lucky chap. Rides like a jockey, what? Don't she?" Exhausted by his exertions, Uncle Beau fell back and sipped gratefully at his whisky. Aunt Milly nodded at him approvingly, the net from her hair, now artfully falling in front of her face, trembling in support.

I discerned that Kerry had cheerfully reconciled herself to the odd relationship between Uncle Beau and her mother. She seemed to treat them with an amused and gentle kindness and remained unembarrassed, despite her mother' recurring screeches of admiration for Uncle Beau. Milly declared archly that, since Beau was so well turned out tonight, she had quite set her cap at him, and did we not think he was too handsome. The fact that he was being pursued with a view to matrimony quite escaped the old boy in his well-oiled haze of bonhomie and general goodwill. He nodded off from time to time, but was generally willing to come to with a loud harrumph, to placate Auntie Milly by patting her and taking a sip or two from the glass she replenished with tender concern. James seemed amused, letting Kerry know that he approved of her gentle acceptance of the two old people, by responding to her with warmth and, presently, falling into protracted and animated conversation with her. I began to see that they were talking with the familiarity of acquaintances.

My mother steered Peter and me away and we became occupied with the greetings and congratulations which rained on us as we moved from group to group, my mother displaying the firm social grace that had made her so famous with the bridge and charity fundraising set. There was an awkward moment when Kicker apprehended that James was addressing him. James simply offered sincere felicitations and returned to his obvious enjoyment of Kerry. I could not help noticing, once again, how often and how closely he bent his head towards hers to hear what she was saying in the general hubbub. Kerry was as demure and self-effacing as she had been when at Wykeford, but I could see, in the flow of years behind us, she had become a pretty and stylish woman. I had to extinguish a ridiculous feeling that perhaps I should not have put the two together.

Peter responded to the increased pressure of

my hand and led me to the dance floor. "Ladies and gentlemen, a tango for the engaged couple," announced the bandleader to a smattering of applause from friends and family. Dancing was something I enjoyed as much as I enjoyed riding, and it was the one thing for which Peter, handsome, blond and still very athletic, shared an equal enthusiasm. I knew from experience he intended to let our skill be seen. It is a moment that will remain forever etched in my mind, however blurred all the other recollections get. We swept into the first showy steps of the tango, laying it on fully, to the obvious pride of Kicker and the amusement of my mother, who loved to dance herself. It was a wonderful, heady physical moment of joy, this effortless tangible synchronicity between Peter and me, our bodies patterned not only in time with the wild elation of the music but with each other for a change. I felt a celebration of recognition in the people, so dear to me, around us. Peter and I stopped in perfect accord with the abrupt cessation of the melody and bowed theatrically, laughing and joking, breathless from exertion.

I straightened up, and looked full into James's face, seeing the same hunted shadowed look I had seen that night I had almost succeeded in getting him to kiss me in the stable before Kicker had cut him with his riding crop. A large triumph swept over me and I smiled, still panting from endeavour, full of fierce wild joy. Then I saw Kerry looking up at James. She was in love with him... I could see it in her face. She would wait for him, however long it took. Whatever he had left after me, she would wait for with patience and grace. She would take whatever he would give her.

CHAPTER SEVEN

How did it feel to be marrying Peter? Well, Anna, it was a marvellous interlude, a conflicting interlude... a time of rediscovery, of slight apprehension and, yes, of some considerable anguish. The confusion of feelings I experienced at that time sent me ranging out across the fields of Heritage. On each of the days between my engagement and marriage, I rode as hard as I could, for as long as I could, under the cloud-laden canopy above Mount Edgecombe, through the rustling, waving silvery green cane. Then out along the skyline, into the light of the sun rising, the sun falling, the sun ablaze in my head and on my body, until its radiance lifted me back into the wheeling of the hadedahs and I could breathe again.

I seemed to need to revisit the haunts of my childhood, as if to say goodbye to myself as I was, knowing the sense of place that had defined me was slipping away as I became something else. I was becoming someone different... someone's wife, someone else's idea. I would not again be able to thunder through the cane on my favourite horse, doing just as I pleased and I tried to compensate for this desperate restlessness by drinking in the wild beauty of the place, hearing a haunted cracked melody from the hadedahs as they picked their way through the fields. I could not subjugate the sense of being confined, no matter how I tried. A new set of expectations and duties seemed to trap me in subtle matrices of doubt. I spent more time than usual out in the fields, delighted to be recognised by some of the cane cutters after so many years and, indeed, stopping to share a plate of breyani where it was offered, savouring it, savouring the days.

In the grand tradition of the Whitneys, my father organised a celebration for the several hundred workers he ruled over as colonial patriarch, my mother providing a feudal feast of huge copper pots, filled with delicately spiced mixtures of rice and vegetables prepared by the maids and numerous vats of juice and alcohol hauled into place by the stable-hands.

Lights, strung across the trees flanking the lawns, had just begun to glitter in the gathering darkness when I came out of my room and crossed the veranda with Peter and my parents in honour of the occasion. Our major domo, Krivahnen Pillay, had just put the finishing touches to the linen-covered tables and I could see the grooms feverishly arranging fireworks that would, later that night, explode across a glowing sky. The cane labourers, their women and children, superbly and exotically dressed, began to clap in unison as we walked down the veranda steps towards them. They shouted approval and congratulations and ribald remarks. Kicker put his arm around me and led me to the table of honour and Peter kissed me soundly to a roar of approval and suggestive remarks as we sat down. The red hibiscus flowers and their deep green leaves made shadowed patterns on the white linen. I knew they had been arranged with special care for me. I smiled at Krivahnen and he bowed slightly.

In front of us, the setting sun poured out a flood of copper on night's black sari swirling along the edges of the horizon. Above us an incandescent moon emerged like an immense gilt-red broach with just a hint of the brilliance it was going to assume during the course of that evening. I felt overwhelmed. Life was so large, so very incandescent. It was difficult to take it all in. I realised that the time for tears was commencing and that it was the moment to say goodbye, to take leave of the things I had known. With regret, I was leaving behind what had always been, with pleasure that I had known such love, such splendour.

Kicker had discerned my intermixture of sadness and he was kind and attentive... a little gruff, if truth be told. My mother, who had been hard at her preparations all day, smiled at me and I saw that she was, herself, dealing with a conflicting set of thoughts. As Kicker rose to make the speech expected of him, I reached under the table and sought her hand.

"I do love you, my girl," she whispered.

"Thanks, Mum," I managed to get out, and I saw how brilliantly her eyes glittered in the flickering of the candles. I loved her so much. Peter sat beside me, solemn and respectful, tolerating our Whitney traditions and ways, but I could feel him masking his impatience, drinking steadily as usual. He was subtly waiting for everything to finish. He wanted to get me out of this, to have me as he pleased, part of his ways and his patterns.

Krivahnen announced the giving of the gifts, and one by one, each plantation family laid a token of esteem on the table before us. Eventually Kicker, my mother and I stood up, reaching out our hands across the table, grasping slender, delicate, fine-boned brown hands in ours, as, one by one, we took leave of each other. I was profoundly glad that I had been here, been part of this great enterprise. All of us here had been woven together in a bond of affection and respect, a bond which had clothed us and fed us well - grown of hard words, toiling struggle, of disappointments, success, of anger, of joy, of gratitude... of gratitude.

As the last of the guests filed by, a musician began to strum a plaintive, complex tune mirroring the ambivalent mood that had settled upon us. Two Indian women in shimmering saris rose to dance out a pattern of precise movements and astonishing grace, their faces rapt and full of dreams. A floating candle in each upturned palm stayed locked in time and space, as their heads and feet wove in and out of the flickering light. It was an ancient homage to love, to passion and the erotic joy of marriage. Brass anklets tinkled out accompaniments to a strangely discordant, beautiful melody plucked from the strings of a sitar. I was caught up in their immersed visions and recognised, with a slight shock, that one of the dancers was the young woman who had waited for her lover, the one I had stumbled upon outside the temple so many years ago. As their beating feet came to a simultaneous rest with the last dying echoing notes, in the moments before Kicker announced the serving of supper, I heard a sweet piping beneath the music. The tree frogs seemed to be weaving their own melodic leitmotif into the night but their clear sounds were soon submerged by the clamour of voices and laughter as the drinking and eating began.

Late that night, I lay across my bed, scenes of celebration flowing through me. I could see exploding fireworks lighting the skies with arcs of intricately woven coloured sparks and I could not stop thinking about the fluidity and grace of the dancing woman. Impressions of the sun-washed walls of the old Hindu temple began to float through the swirl of colour and music in my mind. There had been nothing hesitant about her this night. She was patterned on rituals now, caught, preset, trapped in the steps of the dance.

There was a discrete knock. It was Kicker. He sat down at the foot of my bed.

"Can't you sleep, Joss?"

"No, Dad."

"It's a strange time, isn't it?"

"Yes, Dad. A bit." Kicker felt for my hand.

"You, okay with this, girl? It's not too late to change your mind, you know."

"I don't think changing things will improve anything, Dad," I said evenly.

"It's natural to have doubts at a time like this, Joss. Quite natural."

I sat up and put my arms around his broad back. He placed his hand upon my head and rocked me as if I was a little girl.

"I love you, Dad."

"I know, Jossie, I know. Thank God for it."

I considered Kicker's words. James came to mind, then a vision of my mother's habitual mask. It *was* too late to change things. A subtle cage had been woven around me for most of my life, bringing me to this point, this event. She had woven it. She and Edward Whitney. And Kicker. But I was not my mother. I was ready for Peter, ready to take on marrying him. Changing things would create confusion... we would irrevocably change others if we did, just as they had us. Finally exhaustion overcame my restless musing and I fell into a dreamless sleep, resolving that whatever came my way with Peter, I would not, would never, make my mother's mistakes. I do not know when my father laid me down that evening to return to the bed of his own marriage and it was the last time, but one, I remember my father holding me like that, like a child, rocking me backwards and forwards. He was, with his power and his strength, banishing the many-limbed gods with trunks like elephants, holding off for one last time my haunted dreams of shadow and light.

CHAPTER EIGHT

The day before the wedding dawned sultry with sea heat and a stirring south-westerly, the weather seeming to reflect the hurried final preparations and consultations in crosscurrents of activity. An air of slight hysteria was evident as Kerry, my bridesmaid, and Auntie Milly, a positively crowing matron of honour, helped my mother, bustling about me with pins in their mouths and scissors in their hands, regaling each other with memories of wedding successes and wedding catastrophes. It was wonderful to have Kerry around again and we fell very easily into the camaraderie of our boarding school days. I persuaded her to fetch a bottle of Cape Velvet from the pantry and poured liberal glasses for Milly and my mother. Despite an anchoring ploughman's lunch, the four of us got very merry as the day wore on.

By late afternoon, my mother and Aunt Milly were leaning on one another for support, alternately grave and remorseful at their lack of sobriety, and then overcome with peals of laughter at their inability to behave like decent mothers. As far as sobriety was concerned, Kerry and I were not far behind. It was natural that this state produced in us a period of maudlin confidences.

"I'm in love," said Kerry, waving the empty bottle of Cape Velvet in one hand and a full glass of it in the other.

"So am I," Aunt Milly crowed. Sinking on to the sofa, she unzipped the back of her skirt to gain a little comfort from her substantial lunch, and fell back into the cushions.

"With Beau," explained my mother unsteadily. "I never understood why the two of you broke off your engagement, Mill. You spend enough time chasing him around again in your dotage."

"You were engaged to Uncle Beau!" Kerry and I chorused incredulously.

"Yes, I was. Once." Aunt Milly's eyes filled with tears. "But, then, your mother and I are not too good at walking down the aisle the right man, eh, Johanna?"

"Oh Milly, for God's sake. Don't start on that." I was startled to hear sharpness in my mother's voice. I felt sorry I had been egging them on to match me drink for drink. I had not intended to hurt my mother with reminders, nor Auntie Milly. Milly looked about her, wisps of grey hair escaping her hair net, her small eyes blinking with confused tears.

"Oh dear. Sorry, Jo. I wasn't thinking, lovie."

My mother had instantly regretted her own words and began patting Milly on the shoulder.

"Come on, Mattie. We'd better get to the kitchen and get things going there. Kicker will be here soon... ravenous as usual." Auntie Milly smiled at her and reached around behind herself to tug at her zip, cheered at the thought of being useful to my mother once again. As soon as she stood up and walked to the door, we saw her zip had caught up one of the cushions in its teeth. She was quite oblivious to this fact and the said cushion was flapping up and down behind her as moved forward. Kerry pointed at her and, overcome with laughter, called out, "Ma! Ma!" Milly turned, quite unable to see the cushion. It flipped along with her, bouncing merrily on her buttocks as she moved. At which point, my mother, Kerry and I were totally overwhelmed and began to scream with laughter. Milly twirled this way and that with a balletic grace, but gathering bewilderment, at our inability to explain the cause of our hysterical collapse.

In such a way, Kicker found his womenfolk and supper unattended to. However, I was thrilled to see him responding to my mother's drunken kiss, and he suggested with a wink he might need to take her along to the bedroom until she sobered up. My mother laughed delightedly and I became aware again of how beautiful she actually was, how attractive to men... to Kicker. I felt that vaulting of the heart when she gave me a merry kiss and the two of them left not to appear again that evening. Auntie Milly wound her way off to her room with Kerry in attendance and I was left alone on the veranda with the sinking of the sun before me, a grand and magnificent outpouring. It grew dark and I lay legs thrown across the chair, relaxed and at peace with my lot.

I was startled to hear his voice at the steps.

"Joss? Are you there?" I rose to my feet. It was James. And I knew he should be there... that I wanted him to be there. As with the wheeling skies and the sprawling freedom of space and movement, the privileged position I had held here on my father's plantations, I needed to say goodbye to James too. I needed to place him, along with all the wonder and elation of my childhood, in the treasure chest of my memories. The scattered fig leaves rustled under his feet as he mounted the steps and emerged from the night.

"Joss? Can I see you for a moment?" His familiar voice threw me back across time and I felt I was going to say, as he took my hand, "You know everything, James," and that he was going to laugh and reply in his usual way that there were so very many things we could not know. Instead he placed a small parcel in my hand with obvious pleasure on his face.

"There's something for you before you leave the district, Joss." Light from the lounge windows behind us lit up the small box. My hand was trembling so that I could not unwrap the gift, which made me say, "Shall I open it now, James?"

"That's what's intended, Titch," he answered gravely and took the box from me, extracting a tiny object from the layers of tissue paper which he placed in my palm. In my hand lay a crystal reproduction of a tree frog, perfect in every detail. "This is to remember me by, Joss." I did not know if the points of light it threw off were the result of the light behind me, or of tears.

"Oh, it's beautiful."

"So are you, Joss." I looked up at him and saw what I had not seen before.

"James," I said in a low voice, "Thank you... for this... but you will have to give me something else, something more. You have to get me through tomorrow... and the years ahead, James. You have to..." In the dim light I perceived a look of love, hope, and his hopelessness and resignation.

"What can I give you, Johanna Whitney?" he said. "What can I give you that your mother and my father haven't already taken from me?" I moved towards him and placed my arms around him.

"Oh, James," I murmured, "Oh, James. Kiss me. Please kiss me, James. Hold me... hold me..."

Even now, in the full flood of subsequent years, I still feel the ecstatic, reeling joy when I remember how James finally took me into his arms and kissed me deeply and fully. I do not know how long it was, only that an impossible, brilliant moon had risen along the black edge of night, before we were separated by Aunt Milly's voice folding out of the shadows.

"Jossie, dear, you should be coming in now. Tomorrow is a big day for you." I could not let go of James. He prised my fingers from his and brushed my cheek with the back of his hand.

"It is best so, Joss," he said in a low voice. "We're already determined. It was decided and done, long before all this. If we change things now, only trouble will follow." With that, he turned on his heel and left the veranda, across the shadowed lawns, disappearing into the black light gathering around me.

"Jossie." Aunt Milly had emerged directly from the shadows where she has stumbled upon us. "What's going on?" I drew a shuddering breath and fought to gain control.

"James came to give me a present, Auntie Milly. He came to say goodbye."

"I can see that, honey." I was surprised by the knowing compassion of her voice. "Well, child, I see you're another Nel casualty... like your mother and me," she said matter of factly. In spite of myself, I heard a brittle glasslike pain in her speech, carefully concealed. I heard, for the first time, echoes of sensitivity I had put past her, a ridiculous dithering old woman with her netted hair and crimpolene suits and shameless pursuit of my doltish uncle. She pressed a handkerchief into my hand. "Come, dear. How about a nice cup of tea? We can't have the bride with her eyes all red, can we now? There, there, Jossie... there, there, lovie." She touched my arm and I was grateful for her comfort.

It is strange to me that the mother of my best friend, and my mother's best friend, was the only woman who shared the terrible pain I felt then, which came washing over me in dark rolling waves. But such is the material of existence. Soothing cups of tea and inconsequential conversation holding us together while, internally, we fragment and our worlds fly apart, and we prepare ourselves in agonising darkness to die within. I was glad to have someone to hold my hand while I pulled myself together. This pain emanated from my mother. I had to spend the rest of my life with Peter. I held on to the fact that I would not do, could never do, as she had done. I was strong enough... I was... not to disturb the love that had been created around me. I would not counterfeit by my own selfishness the lives that flowed around me. I was not like her.

CHAPTER NINE

I married Peter Carney twenty-five years ago. Wedding days should dawn fair and bright, in keeping with the verdancy of Mount Edgecombe. The cornucopia of brilliantly backlit sun-risen skies lessened on that day. The immense largesse of light, the generous radiance of the sun, that had poured down on my days as I grew to womanhood amongst the cane fields failed, and steady shafts of drizzle replaced the mist on the morning I arose to become a bride. The wind was rattling my shutters and I could hear the soft cracking of the dry copper fig leaves as they gave up their harvest in sodden immersion. It was a dismal commencement but it ushered in the resolution with which I had retired on the previous night. As I lay listening to the gathering wind whipping up the rain, my mother appeared with a tray.

She began to pour tea into fluted cups. She seemed concerned about me and remarked on the dark rings under my eyes.

"Are you alright, darling? Auntie Milly came to have a chat with me this morning. She was worried about you. Are you fine, darling?" My heart gave a jolt.

"Why, mother? What is she worrying about? Auntie Milly always worries about everything," I said, colour rising in my face.

"Joss," she answered in that helpless, loving way of hers. "Jossie, you can change things if you want to, darling."

"I'm sorry about the weather, Mum. It looks like it's going to spoil things. Don't worry. It's fine. It will clear up. Really." Mute appeal held her face in a matrix of angles and planes. She was a lovely woman, my mother, actually.

"Let's have breakfast now, Mum." She bit her lip and, when she picked up her cup, a little tea spilled from its delicate edges. I put my hand on hers and was pleased to feel the warm fragrant pressure of my mother's fingers as she lifted my own to her cheek.

The rain drummed on into noon, rapping a tattoo on the corrugated iron roof above me, above the metal ceilings that had sheltered me and my dreams and nightmares my whole life. When she left the room, I could not help wondering if she had felt the same on the day of her marriage to Kicker. Had she felt the same apprehension? The same regret? Had she been happy as she gazed into the mirror to brush her hair for the occasion? Or had she had similar lines of eluded sleep shadowing her eyes I now noticed edging my own? Did she, like me, spend the hours before her wedding wondering if she would ever again feel the same soaring, reeling joy, the shocking ecstasy brought by love's first kiss, Edward's kiss? I was so like her, so like her. I brushed my hair mechanically, caught up in that time and place when a woman crosses the threshold of her innocence, and becomes her mother for the very first time.

I remember the church, how it seemed to rise out of the rain as Kicker and I arrived, and how he sheltered me from the worst of the downpour when we stepped across the stone flags into the muted, stained light washing along the pews. Peter waited at the end of the aisle, waited for me to walk past James. I remember looking at my mother, controlling my face as much for me as for her. She held a lace hanky to her mouth and I knew she was crying. Peter wanted to take my hand and steady its ridiculous trembling, so I gave it to him.

And, later, when Peter was sleeping beside me, composed, abandoned... I remember now... that was the very moment I began to know how it was going to be. I was going to have to practise, all my life, the same discipline that had given my mother, Johanna Nel Whitney, her grace and her pain. No matter which way I cut it, I had chosen the road she had travelled. In the face of my best intentions, I had constructed my paths along the lines of her life, and not my own.

The momentum created by the strangeness of a new marriage carried me through, and in time, for a while, I became Peter's good wife. In the beginning I was haunted by a recurring awareness of how things could have been, should have been, but, gradually, my regret turned to resolute endurance. I found that I had a memory of the joy that James had given me so briefly. He loved me, as I did him, and I brought this out into my soul during the darkest times until it stopped hurting and I was able to concentrate on loving Peter, as they both wanted me to.

A stone cottage began to grow out of the craggy valley, clinging to the ridged ribs of Peacevale, a strong thick-walled home, ready for the family Peter and I were keen to begin. Satisfaction grew in me when backbreaking toil produced not only a home, but a garden, springing from the moisture of the small river below us. Peter began to get home later and later from his visits to the club or his games of cricket and rugby, but I was reasonably content, and a flask of tea and a straw hat were all I needed to pass the days away, plastering, painting and gardening. In spite of myself, I grew quite close to Peter's mother Ella in those times. She was reassuringly consistent despite the moments of awkwardness between and, when no baby appeared, someone with whom I could at least talk.

Sometime when night spilled over the crest of the ridge, and the hadedahs flitted like shadowed bats along its edge of failing light, I knew this stone house held me in its clasp and the memories there, as I look back, are imbued with a kind of dark splendour. I would know that Peter would be returning soon; that he would be pushing me against the stony wall and letting me know how he felt about me. There was strange joy in waiting for the flowering of his child within my body. Only sometimes did the shadow of James fall on me, and I would see his face, see him looking into my eyes and saying, "What can I give you, Johanna Whitney? What can I give you that your mother and my father have not already taken?"

The stone cottage walls did not fracture or shift in all the years after it was built. It held fast to its place on the vast granite ridge over which the sunlight spilled while parchment days illuminated and cracked the great rocks above us. The garden grew daily around me, evolving into full-grown beauty, as one season changed into another. But the need arose to fill in the small empty spaces. Peter always stayed to play another game of cricket, or paused to buy another round of drinks. He felt better appreciated in the company of men, more and more at ease in the laughter at the bar, less need to be concerned about me. He came home, eyes glazed, demanding supper, demanding me, too drunk to listen to what I really wanted to say, but not too drunk to notice my instinctive withdrawal... the withdrawal I had learned from my mother.

When his child did not root, the small empty fissures became rifts between us. I would call on Ella Carney because I knew she would invite me in, bustling around the kitchen with a kettle in her hand, opening and closing cupboard doors, and patting the chair at the side of the kitchen table, glad of company to impress.

"You will sit down for a cup of tea, my dear?

You must not worry, Joss. Peter is a good chap. He will do things. This drinking of his is what the men do. You will just have to get used to it. A baby. That is what you need. A baby. That will bring him home froom t'sports club," said with an unnoticed slip of pure Lancashire in her words. I wished I did not have to confide in her but propinquity makes friends of women. Propinquity and need. It brings strange alliances. Later, as I put my head down helplessly on the rickety table and the tears ran between my fingers, she flurried about awkwardly like a trapped bird. "Well, Joss, come now. You'll have to hold up, my dear. We can't have Peter being made uncomfortable, now, can we? He wouldn't like to see you crying," she would say.

I most often waited for Peter on our veranda, watching for him, watching the sky above me shift from rose to maroon before nightfall drew its shutter across the valley, trailing a dusty silver luminescence of stars. I used to hear the hadedahs calling from the ridges and I would search for the dark hooked forms along the last paths of light. I noted, ruefully, how much like my mother I had become - the waiting on the veranda with a tray of tea beside me, the silver tray, the fine white china teapot... and the long hours of inference and supposition. It was the waiting place of my days and months, weaving me into the years. I was sitting just as she had done, not at the edge of rolling fields and wide flat skies above the cane, but encased in a dense granite valley on the veranda of my childless, husbandless home, waiting for Peter. I began to envy my mother. You could set your watch by Kicker's return. Kicker demanded my mother, needed her... insisted on her. As the twilight shadows lengthened into my soul, I would sit silent, abandoned, encased, listening to the hadedahs in the dying of the light. And when their sounds rattled my being and I could contemplate barrenness no longer, I would rise and go to bed questioning their cosmic reeling, and crying their strange harsh cries.

On an evening such as this, I received a call from Kerry.

"Jossie, do you think you could spare a bit of time and drive down to spend a few days with us? My mum wants to see you again and, oh Jossie, I have the most wonderful news." I knew what she was going to say before she said it. " James has asked me to marry him... Jossie? Are you there, Joss?"

"That marvellous, Ker," I managed. Kerry was a lot like her mother in a number of ways. She rattled on. I reached for a chair, feeling faint.

"Do you think you will be able to come down, Joss? I need you to. You being the old married hand. I need you to give me some ideas for the wedding. How about it, Joss?"

"That's fine, Kerry. I'll come down this weekend. Peter's playing cricket at Umtata and I don't really want to go. It will be nice to have some company."

"Isn't it funny how things turn out, Joss? Remember the huge crush you had on James at school. You never used to stop talking about him, do you remember?"

"Yes, it is funny how things turn out."

"Oh, Joss, he's such a wonderful man. He's so kind and I do care about him so very much."

"That's really lovely. Well done. See you Friday."

I put down the receiver and walked to the bedroom. This was my safe haven with its thick stone walls and immense windows. I could see the towering ridge above me faintly tracing the horizon in the darkness, dark and looming, and the sky, rising like a gossamer sari, grey and silver, enfolding it. In the distance the hadedahs called out with a slow enchanted screaming. As I turned from the window, I caught sight of myself in the mirror. The lamp threw shadows and radiance from the walls and caught up me up in luminous reflection. Slowly I began to unbutton my dress, drawing it back from my shoulders.

"Don't stop, Joss." Peter was at the door. "Don't stop undressing, love. You look so pretty." I looked at him in the mirror as he stood behind me. He was hesitant, open. I turned to him deliberately and let my clothes fall to my feet so that he could look at me. A gaze of longing crossed his face.

"I wish this was years ago, Jo. Remember the islands? Remember Greece?"

He drew me to him and caressed the hollow of my neck, brushing my skin with the back of his fingers. He said falteringly, "Are you here for me now, Jo... are you? I miss you, you know. You never really seem as if you are actually here with me." In that instant, I became extraordinarily aware of his own overriding separateness and I was not comfortable with it.

My masks had not been successful. They merely created imitations in him. He was not adept. He had not had my training. This man had his own ghosts to avoid, spectres that shadowed his every day and which belonged to him alone. I became painfully aware that they had everything to do with me. What I was, made him. I was a constant reminder of the roles he did not want to play and, because he had no gift as an actor, he had to seek refuge from the deepest part of me. I was glad that passion began to rise in us. I wanted him to be doing what he was doing... right there... right then.

If propinquity makes friends of women, then it's sheer loneliness that creates the physical bonds between men and women.

CHAPTER TEN

You will want to know about Kerry and James's wedding, darling, since it affected both of us so deeply. Auntie Milly and Kerry lived in a honeysuckle-laden cottage near the Durban North outskirts. Now that I think back, I was particularly looking forward to company. Peter was away so often on weekends. I had had enough of solitude. It was wonderful to have a change of air, notwithstanding the reason for my visit, and for which I had not yet found the ease I desired. Milly threw the door open with cries of welcome when I arrived from Peacevale. I had not forgotten the night long ago she had made her memories available to me, sharing a little of her real self to relieve me of my own burden. She had never said anything to anyone of the time she had found James and me on the veranda. Moreover she had treated me with nothing but kindness, masked by her characteristic dilly-ness. I was grateful. I knew it was silly of me to envy Kerry.

"Hello, Joss," Milly screeched in that crane-like way of hers. "Welcome. Welcome. What do you think of our Kerry? Getting James like that. What a catch! I mean...oh dear..." She recollected herself, realising that she was going down a slippery slope as I had immediately looked down at the floor at these words. "Well now...well now. Here I am, the mother of the bride, and still not married myself," she said archly, attempting to change tone and track simultaneously to our mutual relief. I gave her a hug.

Ducking into the small, cramped lounge, I was startled to see Uncle Beau, the old reprobate, sleeping soundly on the sofa, his socked feet up at one end and the Daily Mercury tented over his round belly.

"Does he live here now, Auntie Milly?" I asked, not entirely innocently.

"Shh," she said, putting her finger to her lips. "Let's not wake him up, poor darling. He'll get the fright of his life. He's not expecting you, dear. His poor wits aren't what they used to be, you know, poor man. It's no good telling him anything. He doesn't remember it… and there's no one to look after him but me." She paused, looking at him fondly. "Who *would* look after him, but me? But you know, lovie, he really should make an honest woman of me. You know how the neighbours talk." Her piercing but contented whisper was enough to raise the dead, never mind alert the neighbours, as to the sinful state of affairs in the house. Uncle Beau slumbered on, perfectly silent and motionless. I smiled at Auntie Milly. She was sweet and well meaning. And I should remember that, I thought, with my inner eyebrow lift. We crept through the lounge to the kitchen where Milly had laid out a milk tart and teacups.

I could hear Kerry coming down the stairs. It was going to be an awkward moment. I must say, Anna, she looked as though she had been dusted in starlight, so bright was the happiness streaming from her. I felt a desperate stab of jealousy despite my earlier resolution. I opened my arms and we hugged each other.

"Kerry! Congratulations, you clever thing." I was pleased to hear how steady my voice sounded. She relaxed perceptibly.

"Oh, Jossie, I do love him. Imagine that. Imagine being the wife of James McKelvey."

"Yes, imagine that," I said lightly. "It's about time too. I'm so pleased for both of you, Kerry." She looked at me uncertainly. "It's the best news, Kerry," I reiterated.

And it was the best thing. It was time to lay the ghosts and settle the ashes. The twin streams of my imagination and reality needed to merge, so that I could flow in a broader river, with confidence, through my own life. Peter needed me. In her maturity, Kerry was a lovely poised woman full of a merry quality that I knew James would never have found in me.

I did wish them well. I did. Time and events have not changed the authenticity of what I thought and felt at that time.

Milly bustled about the kitchen, picking up a tray, on which reposed a single glass of whisky, filled to the brim.

"I must give Beau his sundowner, darlings." She was quite unconscious of the fact that the clock on the wall stood at three o'clock, mid-afternoon. "Don't get up. You'll want to get on with your girls' talk without an old hen like me in the way." She winked conspiratorially and tiptoed off to the lounge. Kerry and I looked at each other across the table.

"You're good with your mum, Kerry," I said. "She's going to miss you when you're gone."

"Thanks. She's got a good heart under all those funny clothes, you know." I nodded. "I used to give her such a hard time, do you remember, Jossie? Oh, Jossie. I'm so happy." She could not keep the joy from her voice. I nodded again, smiling, at which point we were both startled by a sharp wheeze at the door from Milly.

"Oh, dear God," she hissed. "What am I going to do?" Shock and dismay fought for control of her face, her mouth opened to a round "o".

"What, Mum? What? What's the matter?" Kerry sprang to her feet and rushed to her mother.

"It's Beau. Oh. Oh. Oh. Poor, dear Beau!"

"What's going on, Mum?" Kerry asked urgently, shaking her mother in fright.

"Oh, dear. Oh dear. I think Beau has just passed on to a better place. He's so still. So quiet. He won't wake up." Kerry gave a shocked murmur of dissent. Milly sank to the kitchen chair and covered her face with her cardigan.

"Oh, Mum, it can't be! Can it? How can it? He was lying there sleeping a moment ago." Kerry spoke on uncomprehendingly.

"I can't wake him up. Usually I just tap the glass with this little spoon and he's up for his whisky, like a fish for a fly."

"Did you give him a shake, Mum? Is he breathing?" Kerry continued.

"Oh dear Lord, what am I going to do without him?" I was cut to the quick by the anguish on Auntie Milly's face. "What am I going to do?" She pulled a large hanky from her generous bosom and began to dab at her eyes. "Shake him?" she continued confusedly,

"No, I can't shake him. He'd get his death of a fright." I felt a macabre desire to burst into hysterical laughter.

"Well, is he breathing?" Kerry asked insistently, giving her mother another panicked shake.

"Darling, he usually makes a dreadful noise with that snoring sinus of his. You can hear if he's breathing a mile away! Oh dear heart, I'm always complaining about his noise and now there'll be no snoring any more. Oh dear me, oh dear, dear Beau, why did you have to go so?" Auntie Milly began to wail forcefully.

"Get a hold of yourself, Mum. This won't help him!" Kerry shook her mother again Aunt Milly looked up, quivering with sorrow.

"Help him!" she said pathetically, "There's no help for him now, not where he's gone, poor dear soul. Called on to better service… he's left me… alone in the vale of tears, he has. Oh Beau, oh Beau, what am I going to do. You should have married me while there was time, you should have!" She began to weep loudly and helplessly.

Kerry decided to give the old man some assistance, dead or no. She grabbed my hand and we entered the lounge. There was neither movement nor sound from his reclining body.

"Well, let's see to him," I said not relishing the thought. By now I was frightened and did not want to take on the task of assessing Uncle Beau's medical condition. Milly followed hard on our heels, wiping her eyes and sobbing gently.

"No, girls, no. If he's to be seen to, he'll be seen to by me. I won't have anybody else closing his poor dead eyes for him," she said brokenly. The fact that Uncle Beau's eyes were already firmly closed seemed to escape her.

She tiptoed to the sofa, bent over Beau, and then thinking the better of it, rushed back to the door.

"What if he is alive, girls, and I give him a shake. That'll kill him for sure? His poor old heart will never stand such a fright!"

"Check if he's breathing, Mum. Hurry," Kerry said insistently.

"Oh," said Milly, "I'll take this little mirror here and hold it to his nose. That'll show us if he's breathing, hey?" She tiptoed back to the supine man and carefully held the mirror to his open mouth.

"Harrumph! What's this, m'gel? Whisky, m'gel, where's me whisky!" Stirred to revival by the smell of the liquor that had spilled onto Auntie Milly's trembling fingers just a few minutes before, Uncle Beau sat up suddenly, blinking and snorting. Auntie Milly gave a piercing scream and dropped the mirror on the floor, causing Uncle Beau to return to full possession of his faculties, such as they were, instantly.

"Good God, man, Woman! Wot's up here? Y'll give me a heart attack! Wot 'r y'doing, silly coddle?" he said crossly. Milly continued to scream loudly until we had settled her, with her own glass of whisky, on the sofa next to Beau.

"Oh Beau. Oh Beau," she repeated brokenly. "I thought you had gone and left me. I'd be all alone in this world, if you went. All alone." She took a grateful sip of her whisky.

"No chance 'f that, m'gel. Th're a few bottles of whisky left 'n this world to be drunk by none other than ol' Beau here. Never you mind, now, gel... there... there..." he said soothingly.

Beau seemed rather pleased that he had evoked such a response in the old lady beside him, giving me cause to ponder on the fact that in every relationship, no matter what, people needed each other. The idea of being without someone, anyone, was so bad, so appalling, it drove us all to cling frantically whatever soil we found to root in, I thought, looking at the two of them. Oh, how much I have learned since then about people... about myself.

Looking back at Kerry's wedding, I remember a number of other details very clearly. In fact, a newspaper cutting I clipped from the Sunday News the day after Kerry and James got married, fills in some of the points I may have forgotten. Look, you can see it here.

<u>Sunday News 19 Dec 1976</u>

A WEDDING TO REMEMBER

It was a wedding to remember. The highest echelon of Mount Edgecombe society assembled yesterday to celebrate the nuptials of James McKelvey (36), chief executive director of the Tulman Hewgard group, and his beautiful bride, Kerry-Anne D'Unienville (25), daughter of Mrs Millicent D'Unienville and the late Clifford Aston D'Unienville.

The groom's parents, Edward McKelvey, chairman of the North Coast Sugar Association, and his wife Sarah, herself a doyenne of North Coast society, seen here at the reception, were on hand to receive more than several hundred guests. Mr Beaumont Whitney accompanied the bride's mother.

Mr James McKelvey garnered almost as much attention as his lovely young bride, beautifully attired in a Herald Arbentz creation of white satin and ivory detail. As head of the group, the younger Mr McKelvey has taken over from his father in everything but name, wielding considerable influence in the day-to-day affairs of the sugar industry.

The reception, held at the Country Club, after a short ceremony at the Durban North Methodist church, was one of dazzling perfection, noteworthy as much for the superb catering as for the huge number of guest,. Mr and Mrs Kiernan "Kicker" Whitney, (third and fourth from the left), accompanied by their daughter and son-in-law, Mr and Mrs Peter Carney, were among them. All Tulman Hewgard divisions were well represented.

I had been startled to find that my parents were attending the wedding. Kerry's elegant invitation, understated and beautiful, was lying in the silver tray on the mantelpiece in the hallway of my parent's home. When I asked my mother if she would be going, she coloured slightly and nodded. "Kicker's agreed that we should go, since you're the matron of honour, darling." I recall smiling and saying, "How things do change, Mum, don't they?

Even the force of a family feud spends itself… pulls everyone to pieces, then goes somewhere else, just like cyclone Des Moines, hey?"

"You have to let things go, Jossie," she said gently. When my mother rejoined with further light bantering, I had the grace to be sorry for my words. I had probably hurt her again.

It was from Heritage that the entire family departed to accompany Auntie Milly, mother of the bride, to the church. The house was filled with an assortment of distant relatives who shared kinship with Auntie Milly and Kicker, and who caroused with Kicker until all hours, and Joburg and Cape friends, looking for hairdressers and boutiques.

Auntie Milly was in her element and, by dint of much persuasion, we had managed to confine Uncle Beau to no more than two glasses of celebratory liquor in view of the fact that he had to give Kerry away. As a result, he appeared remarkably clear-eyed and steady that day and I remember the debonair air with which he pinned a corsage to his lapel, whistling, *I'm Getting Married In The*

Morning. He kept winking at Auntie Milly whose hair net, sparkling with sequins for the occasion, seemed to tremble in anticipation of a declaration from him at any moment. She was looking quite pretty, having been restrained from her own excesses of powder and rouge. She exclaimed, with a gentle scream, how good it was of Peter to be driving darling Beau to the church to give Kerry away on behalf of her poor dead father.

Oh, and I ache when I remember how beautiful Kerry was as she walked down the aisle, Uncle Beau marching firmly and proudly beside her, how James turned to look at her in a shimmering, shining flush of satin and lace. And my Aunt Milly's sobbing, enjoying to the hilt her moment of glory. And I remember how everything blurred a little in the stained glass splendour, until the feelings that had caught me unawares by the throat, subsided. I also remember my mother patting her eyes with a small dainty square of laced hanky, crying, as all women do, each time one is handed from one man to the next in that essential ritual cycle - familial obligation, duty, procreation and, just sometimes, for reasons of love.

Perhaps more clearly than these memorable, but common, details, I recollect one thing with startling clarity, Anna. When the cake had been cut and the toasts drunk, and the formally arranged patterns of social rank disturbed by the intermingling movements of friends coalescing toward each other in their usual untidy ad hoc groupings for drinking and conversation and laughter, chairs pushed this way and that, half filled glasses forgotten in clouds of conviviality, my mother found herself standing, quite randomly, behind Edward McKelvey. She had left Kicker in the great crowd, roaring out the merits of his horses and his women to gentlemen acquaintances drinking as copiously as only he could, to join the queue at the buffet.

They, my mother and Edward McKelvey, did not know that I was behind them, astonished, intrigued and aghast that such random patterns had brought them together after all their years of careful separation. As he turned, aware all along that she had been standing there, he said simply, "Hanna." My mother's hand flew to her throat and she placed her plate on the table in the most careful way. In the half-light of the candles, as they shimmered on the splendid brocade-covered table, half turned as she was so that I could see her face, I knew. I knew that all the intervening years, all the terrible moments of discipline and control, of appalling denial, had not changed anything. My mother loved this man with all the extent of her being. Nothing, absolutely nothing, had changed that.

"Hello, Edward. How are you?" she said in her clear, precise voice but I could see how the hand she placed in his in greeting trembled. Then she let go of his fingers, and, noticing me, drew me forward.

"May I introduce you to my daughter Joss? You remember Mr McKelvey, don't you, Joss?" Edward McKelvey drew in an audible breath, as his eyes let go of my mother's face, and he brought up his hand once more to shake my own.

"Good God, Hanna. She looks just like you," he said.

Caught up in a crisis of revelation, I closed my eyes for an instant, fighting for control. They began to talk inconsequentially about the drought and the Argentinean polo team's performance. Presently my mask came down as well, and I was able to listen to their conversation with a measure of decorum. However, when it was time to move on, Edward put down his plate and grasped my mother's hands between his own.

"It was good to see you again, Hanna. It was really very good."

"Do give Sarah our regards," my mother said very steadily and politely. "You should join us for a drink one of these days. Tell her to give me a call so we can set it up." I noticed my mother had not removed her hands at all. Edward seemed to collect himself and, dropping his hands to his sides, smiled at her. I was dazzled by the blaze of joy that rose in her face. There are some things people cannot hide and love is one of them. Then he turned on his heel and disappeared into the crowd. This was the man who had usurped Kicker, taken my mother, and James, from me. A river of pity and love for Kicker coursed through me. And for Peter. And for Peter.

My mother stood uncertainly at my side.

"So now you know, Jossie," she said. My eyes filled with tears.

"Oh, Mum, it's so hard to love somebody who may not love you," I whispered. She put her arms up around me and laid her face against mine, and I held her there in the madding, roaring crowd. There were so many questions I had for her, so many things I wanted her to straighten out for me, but I could not ask her there and then. She already had enough to deal with. After that, the moment was lost and, once again, we could no longer talk about this most essential knowledge between us.

CHAPTER ELEVEN

I have another invitation here amongst all these old clippings and letters. You'll be interested in this one, Anna. Can you see there's a photograph attached to it? Dean Edward McKelvey at six months, ready for his christening. Do you recognise him? James and Kerry had been married about four years when he was born

Thinking about it now, those were protracted years... a time of feeling that I had been encased in granite. After their marriage, I had gone back to the valley and taken my existence up with Peter as usual. There were periods of sunshine, to be sure, of an acceptance of things. None of us can sustain a prolonged awareness of the building calamities in our lives. The potential for tragedy is always there, surely, but we seek the relief of ordinary days, visits to the shop, scones for tea, conversations about crops and animals, just so that we do not have to live with too much of that intensity. Peter and I became comfortable with each other, sheltered within tolerance and habit, and, just sometimes, a blaze that amounted to something like happiness. I understood his needs. He knew I was faithful, dependable.

I longed to ask my mother the questions that had sprung to my mouth that night when fate had brought her and Edward, and me, into brief juxtaposition - a juxtaposition just long enough to bring me to understanding of my mother's suffering, but insufficient to tear down the façade between us. I wanted to deal with my own pain, yet I could not add to hers. I was afraid of what I would find. That there would be no resolution, but an impenetrable closure of things for her and for me and that we would never be able to return to the love we shared between us as mother and daughter... however imperfect we were. Was this man Edward my father? I did not dare ask. Perhaps she would say yes. Perhaps she would say that his blood ran in my veins, and in James's, and I could not bear it. I still loved James. I still wished, in unbidden moments, for the feel of his body against my own. There was nothing I could do about that.

Tucked away in that valley, surrounded by the towering rocky ridges with only the soaring of the hadedahs above me, I seemed to rust into base metal and elemental existence. There was a weathering of me, an acquiescence that came upon me slowly, infinitesimally, a settling and, as the months turned into years, a softening of the edges within me, perfectly reflected in my face. I was aware, when I looked at myself in the mirror, that I had inherited her mask. Clearly imprinted were the matters closest to the inner walls of my heart, but, never expressed, never uttered, they were merely the form on which speculative questions settled. But this masquerade was not my mother's graceful, practised social one. My face was not contained in anything that fortunate. What I distinguished were the granite etchings of resignation.

Not that I became reclusive. Life thrust itself into the passing moments. I did what I should. I had tea with Peter's mother and sister on a regular basis and discussed, brightly, the substance with which they were comfortable, the issues that they did not wish to avoid, the perimeters they were prepared to contain. I visited Kerry, dandled Dean on my knee. I saw my mother and Kicker from time to time. We had tea, we had lunch, attended the theatre. But all the while that slow dissolving, that still slipping into the years of one's existence.

I used to sit in the wooden chair on our veranda, waiting for Peter, watching the glow of radiance along the edge of the Peacevale cliffs fade into dark oblivion. I was faintly aware of bush pig in the rustling undergrowth but, lost in the wild heady perfume of flowering jasmine, was unable to do anything but continue wrestling with my stubborn psyche, which refused to let James go. That brought grace. Wrestling brought control. But at such times my thoughts were alive with him, with reminiscences of how he used to be, the things I remember him saying... the feeling of his hand on my waist... the knowledge that his father had held my mother in much the same way.

On one of these nights, in the half-light of valley and cliff shadow, a series of events occurred which lifted me very suddenly from my long reverie and changed, quite drastically, the course of all our lives.

The wind had flicked through the trees for days. Intermittent and sullen rain had poured torrents of water into the valley. Twenty-five years or more on, I can still hear in the auditorium of my memory the uncomfortable shifting of restless branches, whipping about with increasing intensity. Moisture-laden, the wind tossed the trees backwards and forwards, backwards and forwards. It was later than usual for Peter to be coming home. I began to worry about the treacherous road along the edge of the valley. I knew if Peter had had rather more than usual at the bar that night, a misjudged turn would hurtle him in his old Land Rover several hundred feet

118

into the river below. I do recollect being angry with Peter for making me anxious with his drinking and I know that when I went resolutely to bed, sleep eluded me for several hours.

It must have been some time after midnight that I was jerked awake from an uneasy slumber. A violent series of lightning cracks ripped me into full consciousness and I jerked up in terror. Vehemently splintering, glass spat from window panes into the air as lightening struck the veranda repeatedly. In this suddenly unfamiliar night it was too dark to see and a terrible keening spilled from the storm that had suddenly assailed the cottage.

Briefly, at the edge of consciousness, I heard Peter shrieking my name over and over again. In his voice was a terrible note of panic. Emerging from the house into the engulfing darkness, I found rain beating into my blind face with staggering force. I struggled to find my bearings. The wind had risen to a razor-edged howl of storm and I could just hear

Peter's continuing cries above the obscure, awful roar of a river in full flood.

Normally placid, the stream that fell through the valley walls with a meandering beauty had gathered in the storms from the Drakensburg Mountains. In screaming, swollen fury, whipped by the cyclonic force of the storm, it was sweeping everything in its path aside. The bridge of solid granite we had built cross the stream at the valley's foot had burst apart under this onslaught, the cyclone throwing most of its force at us. I felt as if the eyes had been gouged from my head in the shrill intense rushing darkness and gasped as the rain beat into me with astonishing coercion.

Peter must have tried to drive onto the bridge, not knowing it had begun to give way. I tried desperately to see what was happening. "Peter! Peter! Where are you?" I shrieked. The noise was so overwhelming, I could just make out his desperate calling.

"Jossie! I'm on the bridge. It's taking the rover with it. I'm caught. Get some rope! Get me something to hang on to. Hurry! Hurry!" Peter was in immense danger.

I heard Peter call again, and, then, an ominous grinding of slipping boulders. One by one, they began to detach themselves from the remaining edifice of the bridge. I saw him, then, clinging to the edge of the tilted vehicle in the oily, shimmering, boiling water. All the while the deluge sucked at the fractured bridge and great fuming remnants of storm debris battered against it in the steadily rising river. Peter would be swept away if he let go. He was cold and exhausted and the terror that rose in me that he was going to die was darker and more threatening than the sinister darkness into which we had been hurled with little warning.

"The rover's slipping. Get me some rope, Jossie! Some rope." I rushed desperately towards the house, searching for any rigging lain along the edges of our garage. The lights were gone. I ran my hands along the splintered shelves in the fractured shadows, desperately feeling for anything that would help. My fingers finally located thick oily rope coils. I could barely pull the tangled cords apart, but I came upon an old tyre tube underneath them, devoid of air, but sufficient for the need at hand. I managed to tie rope to rubber with thick hasty knots and pulled the rope from the garage.

Through the dim illumination of a sheet of intermittent lightning, I dragged the rope along in the drowning wind and began to climb up against the side of the valley, slipping and falling. The wind seemed to wind up a pitch, as if spinning on a gyre. In its devastating clamour I could no longer hear Peter.

"Peter!" I screamed, "Peter, I'm throwing rope down. Peter! Watch out for the rope." I reached the bank above the bridge and pulled one end of the rope through the forked branch of a tree. "Here it comes, Pete. Try to feel for it. Peter! Peter, can you hear me?" The tube at the end of the rope bucked wildly as it hit the water and then, snagging in floating debris, swept around the bend. I had not attached the rope securely enough and it was slipping away. I wound my arms around the tree, snatching the rope end as it skidded through the cleft in the branches. Suddenly it wrenched taut, pinning my arms into the hard bark of the trunk. The rope began to hold. I heard Peter again and began screaming into the baying wind, the rope riddling the flesh from my wrists, exposing bone and sinew. Grinding and tearing, the granite base separated from the framework of the bridge and, together with the tilted vehicle, slid away grating and shifting into the raging stream.

As you know well, Peter did survive. He managed to haul himself in, one hand after the other along the rope, using his last vestiges of strength to ward off the battering stumps and whirling branches the flood had torn down from the river banks and was flinging wildly at him. I remember how he fell forward at my feet on the muddy bank, utterly spent. Then, he was pulling gently at the rope, picking the strands from my flayed arms, saying over and over again, "My God, Jossie, look at your hands. Look at your arms. My God. My God." And I remember thinking that he looked terribly bruised, terribly battered, as he said it.

The flood took the farm with it. It stripped the valley bare of everything we possessed and left the most terrible scars, bringing to a standstill the little money we had been making. Only the stone cottage stayed immovable, unyielding sentinel to our destruction. And, although Peter began almost immediately to restore the damaged lands, I saw that the cyclone had taken away his courage, and his passion. After that he seemed to spend even longer away. Even before my arms had healed, he took to drinking harder and heavier than before. He seemed darker, more sombre, lonelier than ever.

Finally, despair caused me to leave the valley. When I told Peter I had taken a job teaching English in Kloof, he put his fist through the door. I did try. Oh, I did try, I tried so hard to do right by Peter, to love him in a way that the shadowed hadedas of knowing something different would cease to flit between us. But I could not make up for him the sense that he was incomplete, the feeling he was not enough... that he wasn't James.

I've spent a quarter of a century living with the events and consequences of that night, and I find there's no profit in searching for places to lay guilt, Anna. It's enough to have to deal with remorse without having to participate in the apportionment of blame and retribution. We need no judges, Anna. We sentence ourselves, girl. This anguish is punishment enough for what we do... it's enough... it's enough to have to live with memories and recollections... without having to pay for them as well. Truth is never assumed, Anna... only apprehended.

CHAPTER TWELVE

The large school where I was to teach for the next four years was disciplined, ordered and well run. Behind the bougainvillaea-laden entrance gates and crowded staff car park was a busy, self-focussed world of predictable regularities and small parcels of recurring carefully timed periods that suited me tremendously. I found a haven there in the busy pressure, an anonymity where I mattered only to the clamouring, changing children I taught. I cared for them greatly. They were a demanding, complicated, rumbustious substitute for my own lack of children and at night when I got home to the empty silent stone cottage in the valley I was too tired to care about being on my own.

The first months passed in a haze of exhaustion, until I began to adjust to the physical and mental strain of teaching, and started enjoying the long days of standing, exhorting and motivating, of being endlessly available, being constantly and completely necessary to the scheme of things. The small victories of teaching and learning to teach added up imperceptibly until a larger picture of shaping and moulding, leading and directing, a moving towards value and meaning, emerged for my young charges and for me. I was tremendously grateful for that.

It was a time of flutes and hymns. The days passed into an endless summer of radiant light on sweeping, green, clipped fields where young people threw balls, and dingy dirty classrooms where they explored the dimensions of intellect for the first time as adults. Here there were no large consequences, only a certainty of life's endless possibilities. I began to seek friendship in the camaraderie of the staff room and was delighted to find myself accepted, sometimes, even, valued. Peter's retreat into himself, his slipping away into alcoholism and sullen silence, his dis-involvement, did not seem to matter so much somehow, as long as I was caught up by the school's consuming imperative.

I don't know exactly how it began... my affair with Riaan, I mean. Teaching is the kind of work where you are thrown into close contact with people's emotions. It exacts deep personal responses, congruence, plenty of positive regard, the things born of one's close propinquity with other people's psychology, Anna. While it's not supposed to be, a school is a dangerous coalescence of feeling. I remember shying away from him when I began to see a resemblance between him and James McKelvey. He seemed to wander across to the circle of chairs where I sat to grab a hurried cup of tea before the next class often, and I was struck at his openness. He was so willing to talk about his own reactions and feelings. He asked me about everything. Why did I have scars on my wrists? What did I think of the senior mistress? Why was I so quiet? He really was so very Afrikaans.

And, then, one day on the stairs, among the crowds of laughing, noisy teenagers pushing and shoving to the next lesson, he took my books from me and carried them along the corridor, placing them on my desk while I followed him, hesitant, charmed. When he turned to leave the classroom, he looked at me and I knew it was the moment of change between us. In this unexpected longing that rose in me, I fell into a new dynamic. I avoided the staff room and changed the habitual routes of my movements in the large buildings, gathering an undeserved reputation for being "dedicated" as I was seldom at tea. However, a school is a small world and I found myself teamed with Riaan at this gala or that parent's day and eventually one evening, as I hurried away from a long and tedious school function, I found Riaan waiting for me on the steps of the school entrance.

"Why are you avoiding me, Johanna?" he asked evenly. I looked at him wordlessly. He had used my mother's name; the one everyone called her. He said it in the Afrikaans way, with the J sounding like a Y. The earth seemed to rock beneath me in a giddy precessional spin.

"I'm married, Riaan," I said flatly.

"Not happily, Johanna. Not so?" I noticed the warm Malmesbury burr in his voice, heightened by emotion. He was serious and intent.

"That's none of your business, Riaan," I said.

"Ah, but it is, Johanna… it is…"

"Don't say it, Riaan. Don't say these things."

"But I must, liefling." I put my head into my hands. His term of endearment was the sweetest thing. I looked up at him and found myself breathing unsteadily. He was so attractive, so very available.

"I must be going home, Riaan. Peter is waiting for me."

"Don't lie to me." The night seemed to stretch suddenly into eternity, and I was overwhelmed with loneliness and desire. "Please come with me," he said. "Let's go somewhere talk about this," he continued and walked around the car to climb into the passenger seat beside me.

"This is wrong, Riaan," I replied and started the car. "Where do you want me to go?"

Riaan's flat was not far from the school, tucked away in the pretty oak lanes of Winston Park. I was aware of taste and order, rows of books, pencils, riding accoutrements.

"Oh, Riaan, I see you ride. I haven't been out in such a long time," I said. It seemed to relieve the tension between us. He was delighted and picked up an album of pictures so that I could admire the horses he had owned. He fitted a tape into a deck, and Andreas Vollenweider's melodic, elegant harp poured jazz into the air. Riaan poured two sets of gin and tonic and placed a glass in my hand.

"Hey, Joss, you're shaking," he said.

"Yes."

"We're not going to talk about this, are we?"

"No."

"Come here, then, *liefling*," he said, taking me into his arms. His mouth covered mine and I found myself responding with ardour. It felt so good to be desired in this way. The world began to spin again. He knelt beside me and began to unfasten the buttons of my blouse.

Once committed to faithlessness, I fell into a heady time seeking him often, enclosed and full of joy. I recollect walking across the stage of the dim, vast school hall one assembly, after one such night with Riaan, alive with the possibilities of the morning, and catching in Riaan's face a look of pride and flirtation. Outwardly all was the same, but inwardly I lived in a flame of sensual physical knowledge, and the man knew it, and loved it, loved being the cause of it. I smiled at him, settling down in the back ranks and was rewarded with a conspiratorial wink. Then he frowned and looked down at the floorboards, and I was abruptly aware that our liaison was no longer confidential. The senior mistress, watchful sentinel of school morality, had been keeping a lookout for just such a moment and, as the school broke into a dirge-like morning hymn, gave me a look of great significance. I knew I was about to be summonsed.

Miserable hours followed. I did not want Peter to find out about my disloyalty. I knew it would just push him further along his paths of his retreat and I felt unkind to him, and unreliable as a teacher. I had not been open with Peter. I had never been. It was not his fault that I had loved James. How could I blame him for *me* not being strong enough to resist the temptation of temporary joy Riaan had brought? Peter would want to know why I had to be transferred from the school, which is what happened to teachers who behaved indiscreetly with each other. This was part of the unwritten code, unwritten but real. He would have to know. The headmaster was bound to tell him if I did not. My thoughts spun webs of confusion and distress.

Riaan arrived at my classroom door that afternoon, after the pupils had left.

"Listen, *liefling,* this has got nothing to do with them," he said. I shook my head.

"It's not that, Riaan... it's Peter. What am I going to tell Peter?" Riaan impatiently put down the blackboard duster he had picked up.

"Marry me, Johanna," he said, and in that moment I knew I could not. I could not turn Riaan into another spectre and see him wasting away like Peter. I had not thought about James in a long time but he was still there, carved into the interior walls of my heart. I could not make Riaan pay for my own solitary pain, which came rushing back to me as soon as he uttered these words.

"I'm not going to do that, Riaan," I said slowly. "I can't marry you."

"How can you say that, *liefling?* Tell me how? You don't love him."

"Oh, yes, I do," I said even more slowly. Riaan turned from me, utterly confused, and then stopped.

"How can you love a drunk like him, man? How can he be worth it, Johanna? How?" I could not answer. Remorse flooded me for these men, for Peter, for Riaan, for James. I could not hold back my tears.

"Don't worry, *liefling.* Don't worry. We can get through this. It's okay... Please let me see this through with you, Johanna, please..." He said "Johanna" in the Afrikaans way again, with a soft "Y", and I had to hold him, even if someone did return to the classroom and we were found. The school, as I have said, was a very self-contained world.

I left the school at once and drove home to wait for Peter. In the familiar shadows of the veranda from the vantage of my favourite chair, I began to sift through my feelings. Peter did not come home that night, so I did not tell him, and, by the time Riaan had spent several hours the following day talking to me on the phone, I was persuaded to let things stand as they were for the time being. However, the summons *did* arrive during the next day of school, with the most unexpected of results.

I arrived at the Helen Wilton's office and stood waiting at the door, like a schoolgirl, before she called me in. "Sit down, Mrs Carney," she said. I picked up the slightly ironic emphasis on my title as I dutifully sat down. "Mrs Carney, as a high school teacher I should not have to tell you that we rely on you to provide a good example to our girls. Indeed it behooves us to make the right kind of choices in order that that we not bring discredit upon our profession, or upon our school, not so?" Behooves? She sounded exactly as she did when she stood on the school stage lecturing the girls in her charge. I could not but nod agreement. I was grateful for the professional façade that protected both of us right then. This slightly worn, slightly faded woman worked as hard as I did. She cared as much about things as I did. I knew that. I saw suddenly that she was quite lovely. "Riaan Berkhout is a good teacher, Joss. We can't afford to lose him." I nodded again.

"I can go, Mrs Wilton. I won't make it difficult," I said fairly unsteadily. I was surprised to hear her give a sigh of exasperation.

"Oh for God's sake, Joss. Do you think I haven't been through this a dozen times already!" I looked up at her sharply. The mask had fallen from her face and had been replaced by a look of compassion. She had sunk back in her chair, and was watching me carefully. "Teachers are human beings," she continued. It sounded like a cry, coming from her. "We can't afford to lose you either, Joss. You're an excellent teacher yourself. It's not surprising you and Riaan Berkhout have got together. You complement each other." She lifted her hand as I sat forward in astonishment. She was normally so remote, so professionally impersonal. "Yes, it has been apparent for some while. People do talk. Especially here... especially the kids, the rotten little hypocrites... and their parents, too. Everyone can see the man is wild about you. It's clear to me that he can't keep his hands off you." She paused. "What are you going to do about this mess, Joss? You're going to have to end it or marry him. It'll take time, but people do forget in the end, if you marry him, I mean... They tolerate that, but not an affair, not one involving a married woman. You will get hurt in the end. Their talk will hurt you badly."

"I hadn't realised it was that obvious," I said.

"These things aren't always, but in your case neither of you can hide it… and that's not good for the school," she replied wryly, and I noticed, suddenly, that her eyes were filling with her own hurt.

"Mrs. Wilton, are you alright…?" I asked hesitantly. She brushed a wisp of blonde hair from her face.

"Oh, yes. I have an idea of what you must be going through, my dear. Andrew and I have been, ah, involved for years, you know." It was my turn to sink back into my chair. Andrew? The headmaster? Andrew Denton! I was stunned into silence. She smiled her slight smile again. "Occupational hazard. None of us is immune." I felt overwhelmingly grateful to her. I stood up to leave.

"Thanks, Mrs Wilton… for your confidence. Thank you for telling me."

"That's quite alright, Joss. Just close the door when you leave. And Joss… call me Helen, will you?"

I should have had the courage to tell Peter that night, but I didn't. I drove to Riaan's flat after work and waited for him to return from a school outing. When he came in a little after six, I drew him to me. "Make love to me, Riaan," I said, because I wanted to see his face blaze with joy. "Love me, Riaan. Love me," because I didn't want to wear my masks any longer, because I did not want to spend another night alone. "Touch me there, Riaan, now, now," because I didn't want to deal with Peter. And, by eight o'clock, we were spent with passion. He moved me from the kitchen, strewing my clothes along the stairs as we went, across the floor and to the bed... and the bed... You see, Anna, I am so much like you. There is nothing we do not share as women, darling. "You are mine, Joss. You are mine," he said over and over again and my body came up to meet his, and we conceived you, Anna, my dearest, dearest daughter. You began to grow in me that night, began to form yourself in stillness and perfection, for the miracle of your birth.

Peter never knew I had fallen pregnant with you. He died just a few days after I had discovered this for myself. But not before he had found out about Riaan. After he confronted me with the fact of his discovery, with the angry raging words that he'd followed me to Riaan's flat and seen what was happening, he drove away from the cottage in a towering rage. Somewhere along the valley road, he misjudged a turn and the car fell into the river below. They found his broken body after only a few hours of searching. He just left me like that. He never gave me a chance to say sorry. He just left me. Oh, Anna, these are the difficult memories... but, I will tell you... everything.

CHAPTER THIRTEEN

I cannot recollect, now, after all these years, how I felt in the immediate hours after a grave young policeman knocked at the door of the stone cottage and said, "We've found him, ma'am... It took us a while. It's dark out there. We've taken him to the hospital... but the news is not good, ma'am... it's not good..." But I do remember waiting for my mother to arrive after I had phoned her, waking her in the depths of sleep and saying in flat, automatic tones, "Peter's dead, Mum. Please come, Mum. Peter's been killed in a car accident." And I have a clear recollection of how sharply she cried out, "No. No. Oh God, no!" I also remember walking onto the veranda and sitting in my chair, so that I could watch the sun rising from behind the valley ridge, and then my parents arriving, and a little later Auntie Milly, and Kerry and James, and the Carneys, ashen with shock and pain.

They made all the awful arrangements and brought me tea, and tried to get me to eat after I threw up in the bathroom. And Dr Moffat arrived and said to my mother, "I'm loath to give her what I've got on me for shock, Johanna. She'll have to have something to get her through this. I'll get the chemist to send someone out with something more suitable for her condition." I remember the startled way my mother replied, "Her condition?" And the doctor's quiet, gruff reply, "Well, Johanna, this is not an auspicious time to learn about your impending status as a grandmother... but so it is, so it is." He also said, "I'll be off now and do what I have to on the other side. It's a sad business... a sorry one, indeed. I'll stop by and inform the relevant people. Can you get Kicker to come up and identify him? I'll wait for him at the hospital morgue. Try to get her to rest now. Sometimes, a severe shock like this... You will have to be careful. It's been a very long night for her. She must rest."

How I got through the slow long hours before Peter's burial, I do not know. It was as if I had I had plunged into a yawning black chasm of my own making, and, in spinning along the fissures of my falling, become suspended so that I could never again reach the bottom. Caught in the spider web of my dark complicity, I felt the most terrible anguish. Somewhere in those alternating periods of drugged sleep and grief-stricken awareness after Peter had fallen into the valley, I have a vague memory of my mother holding me in her arms and saying, "It's no one's fault, darling. These things just happen, Jossie. They just happen. Don't fret, Joss... try to sleep, darling, try to sleep..."

Kicker was there, too. "Come, sweetheart, sit up now and take a bit of soup. It'll be needed by that little one inside you," and, "What about a walk round the garden with me, love? Come, a bit of exercise will do all of us good." When I walked with him and saw him limping and realised how bowed he was getting with age, I clung to him and cried. He patted me and held me to his shoulder and said, "There, there... a good cry is the thing. Are you okay with this, girl? Can you manage? Come, try to manage." And I remember the hadedahs stitching their evening paths above us, reeling all the terrible pain of existence into themselves, and myself standing at the window and, like them, crying strange harsh cries.

I have reminiscence, also, of my heart lurching when Kerry entered the room and, her sitting on the bed beside me, saying gravely, "Joss, Peter's folks have called again to see how you are. And Mrs Wilton and... oh yes, Riaan from the school." And then, after a pause, "Joss, you didn't say you were pregnant... I'm so glad for you, Jossie. I know it's too soon, but having Peter's little one is going to take you through the years ahead. It's going to fill some of the empty spaces, darling... it will, I promise...Dean's been such a joy." She touched my shoulder as I turned my face to the wall. "Oh God, Joss, I'm so sorry... I'm so very sorry." Presently I took her hand and she went on, "It's okay, really. James says I must tell you we're both on standby for you. That you mustn't worry needlessly. We'll be there for you, both of us.

Always. Don't worry, Jossie, don't worry." And, then, "You'll have to come with me, darling. You need to get some clothes for the funeral. You need to get ready for tomorrow, Joss. Do you think you can manage? I can't find any black dresses in your cupboard."

It takes ritual to assemble fully a cast of family and friends and acquaintances. Peter's funeral was no exception. Apart from immediate relatives, Auntie Milly, with Beau, Kerry, James and a very solemn two-year-old Dean in attendance, arrived in the cortege. Edward and Sarah Whitney stepped down from their elegant car and offered condolences to Peter's inconsolable, utterly distraught mother and pale stunned father and shocked sister. Next, Andrew Denton and Helen Wilton paid their respects. Riaan, frowning in the drifting dust and vivid sunshine, stood solemnly behind them, waiting for an opportunity to say something to me. I saw that Edward had taken my mother's hand in his. James took my hand in just the same way. Then my mother turned to lean on Kicker, and

I was left on my own, and the priest began those most unfamiliar words of consignment to the earth.

This company, which would never again gather around Peter Carney, stood silent, heads bowed, throughout the service. I knew, then, with shocking conviction I would never be able to tell Riaan that I bore his child within me... never be able to tell anyone. Sickening disbelief, dire contrition, rose within me. We approached the side of the grave and I held on to my mother's arm. The faces that looked towards me seemed flayed, stripped of skin. I bit my lip and looked down into the dreadful hole where they were about to place Peter. I could not believe these things were taking place. I would never in my own life be able to make it up to Peter, this thing that I had done. I would have to create some kind of respect for his memory. I would have to remain silent, my guilt unvoiced, forever responsible, forever caught.

I recollect that we moved away from the graveside, disassembling, and reassembling at our home... my home... for the rites of eating and the wakes of drinking that release mourners from their grieving. Then, they can return to the routines and concerns, so abruptly thrust aside by the verity of death. Grief comes in waves, and then recedes, as the days fall like leaves into the garden of years, then bereavement flowers up only intermittently and briefly, with this reminiscence or that. I can't remember him any more. I can't summon up the details of his face... attrition in the descent of years, Anna... Peter stays forever young in my mind, everlastingly troubled and lonely. Oh, Peter, what a bitter, bitter legacy! And yet, and yet... here you are beside me, Anna, beloved daughter. Here you are grown and beautiful, on the eve of your own wedding, and here we sit side by side as mother and daughter, sharing the things that must be shared between us... just as my mother had to share herself with me... and it is time, Anna, long past time.

Riaan did not try to contact me for a long while after I left the school, but I understood why. The guilt of Peter's death had been severe for him too, and I was so obviously pregnant as the school term drew to a close, he must have thought exactly what I intended him to. I knew there was hurt and confusion in him, but I held resolutely to the path I had chosen. I had refused to leave Peter for him before the car accident and its dreadful aftermath, and now he was sure he knew why. And, as for me, I had to get on with things the best way I knew how.

And then, Anna, you were born one wild, starry night when the moon turned the cane stalks to silver and the cane leaves into tossing black shadows. You came to me in my confusion and pain, and when I looked into your barely opened eyes, I saw that wonderful baffled love that you brought with you from the dark stars above us, and which in your helpless immaculate newness, you could not

148

hide. In this strange unaccustomed dependency, mine as well as yours, I found strength and hope. The days began to lengthen and shine again, strewing panoplies of careless flowers and radiant moments, and sudden joy, into the dark seedbeds that constituted the walls of my heart.

You were, as all babies are, beautiful beyond every one of the parameters of my previous knowing - loving, engaged, and insistent. You revealed, in your very assertion, the meaning I had been unable to derive from that time that James had gone away, taking my nine-year-old heart with him, never to bring back. I had existed in each subsequent moment since bereft and incomplete, unable to understand how the shadows had woven out of such sheen... until I held you for the first time, and found that the shadows themselves could yield a marvellous and radiant pattern. Oh, Anna, how very much like their mothers daughters are!

The months went by, I grew stronger, more able to examine my part in Peter's death without feeling I was plunging into an abyss from which there could be no return. Just sometimes, at night, I would start up in terror, convinced I had heard Peter calling, over and over again, from the other side of the river, and then I would find I was in my own familiar room in Mount Edgecombe with its metal ceilings and slowly revolving roof fans. And find you beside me with your small soft breathing and tiny movements, and would draw you to my breast and hold you close, so close, to my heart.

You know, Anna, Kicker had you up in a saddle by the time you were three. You learned to ride as well as I did, while your anxious grandmother called out with concerned cries from the white railings of the paddock and you laughed with pleasure and wonder at the movements of the great horse beneath you. My parents loved you utterly and you brought them great joy. For me, it was the greatest source of happiness just to have you growing there, in the remembered places where my own small being had been formed.

There, under the shimmer of the radiant vault which drew its vast clouds across evening into immense starry velvet folds out of the towering, brilliant reds and roses of the dying night, only to blaze up again a few hours later into a dew-ridden morning... that is where you spent your early days, much to my profound contentment. I was deeply satisfied when I saw Krivahnen, beginning to bend with age, starting to be white-haired, fawning after you, a prisoner to your childish charm, in the very same way he'd looked after me. What a safe and beautiful country the country of childhood can be, when it is rooted in continuity and bordered with love.

All the same, I could not loosen the iron grip of Peter's valley from my spirit. It was years before I was released from it. The stone cottage and its now dead garden were a part of my anguish. Their memories held me apart and separate, unable to participate in joy, a reminder of the things I had done. Something was imprisoned within and would never find release. I found it increasingly difficult to visit

Grandmother Ella and Tim. But, when I looked into your bright face lit with insistent flowing energy, there were flashes when my heart beat again with the joyful rhythms and songs that had threaded themselves through the long vivid days of my own youth. How much you brought with you, my darling child.

I spent much time with Kicker. Perhaps the granite that had me enfolded in a deep sense of loss had made it possible to recognise the wellspring of his own stubborn, passionate character. I was drawn to him more and more often. He was finding the management of the plantations heavy going and he no longer sat so comfortably astride a great roan, directing and managing the processes from cane to cut to cane again, the practice which had brought him such wealth. I found myself getting interested in his long rambling evening talks, which revolved around cane and sugar and almost nothing else, and he began to entrust me with standing orders and inspections and, gradually, more and more of the management of Heritage.

152

Long before Krivahnen began beating the dangling iron outside the kitchen door to announce breakfast, I would be up and away, the grooms scrambling to have my mount ready by first light. An hour later, I would return to find Kicker waiting eagerly for me so I could report back on the matters so close to his heart. Production, labour, disputes, planting, cutting, firing, the endless minutiae of cane production... all gradually began to make sense. And then I would be out again, thundering along the cane gullies at full gallop, dismounting to carry out his instructions, and on again to repeat the procedure somewhere else. And that way, I could fall exhausted into bed every night and sink into a dreamless deep sleep where Peter rested too. And so the years fled by.

Oh, Anna, I do remember lying in my own bed in the half-light of the morning and hearing your small voice, "Mama?" and my reply, "Come in, Anna. Come in, darling." You would clamber into my arms and lie encircled, while you drifted into the shining visions of your own secure, enchanted world.

What I remember too of the time when you were six or seven, were the days when Kerry came with Dean, sturdy and manly, all of nine or so, when Kerry and I were becoming firmer and firmer in our amity. The two of you would disappear to find mongoose trails and hunt fish in the stream below, while the fish eagles fluted above us, and Kerry and I would lie on the lawn talking as we used to in the old days of Wykeford.

"You're working too hard, Joss," Kerry would say.

"It gives me something to do, Ker. It's absorbing really. I don't mind."

"Doesn't give you much of a social life, Joss, all this plantation stuff. You're wasting away here. What about joining me and James at the club on Saturday?"

"Mmm... doesn't really appeal. Truly, I'm happy here. I like being with Mum and Dad."

"You've become singular, Joss. You need to get out and meet a few nice men... no, don't look at me like that... it would do you good to give all this responsibility a rest now and then. You could do with someone in your life... help share the load a bit?"

"Ah, Ker, give it a break, will you. I'm okay. Really."

"Well, then... hie, you two, watch out! Anna will fall, Dean! Don't climb so high! Well, as I was saying, Joss, you need to get out and find someone. You'll have to get out the glad rags and come socialising with us, hey, Jossie? When do you think my mom and old Beau will finally decide to do the decent thing and tie the knot?"

"Don't you think our two are spending too much time together, Kerry?" I asked to change the subject. Kerry dismissed this concern airily, after looking at me sideways.

"It's not *their* wedding we're talking about, Joss. But don't you think that would be good... your daughter and my son?" She paused, looking fondly at Dean.

I shifted uncomfortably. Somewhere along the line, the connection between the Whitneys and the McKelveys had to find its end. Look at what I had done to Peter by loving James. Look at what I had done to Riaan. I did not want you to travel these rocky paths, Anna. I vowed there and then your life was not going to be disturbed by the McKelveys. Observing my suddenly closed face, Kerry searched for her words. "We've been friends a long time now, eh, Joss? He'll do for your daughter, Joss. He will... and don't look at me like that! She's growing up, you know. Look at that, will you! That boy is going to give me grey hairs before my time... but he's turned out nicely, hasn't he? "And Dean did turn out nicely, as you know, Anna! Dean was lovely as a boy, in that distinctive McKelvey way. You adored him. You would not hear a word against him, even then. Even then the look of him, the dark eyes, the clean lines of him struck me... and he called you Titch! That was something... the boy calling you Titch, like that. You know, Anna, you thought he knew everything there was to know in the whole world when you were just twelve and he was fourteen going on fifteen.

CHAPTER FOURTEEN

Through those years of friendship with Kerry, my contact with James was minimal except for one or two instances. We led busy lives. I was not in the habit of going out on weekends... hmm... looking back, I suppose I did not seek him out for fear I would get to know him again. I had shut him out of my heart twice before and did not want to have to do it again.

At about that time, there was some acrimony between the smaller sugar farmers, like my father, and the huge sugar conglomerate, which dictated prices and terms, and just about everything else, in the lives of the Mount Edgecombe community. Kicker asked me to accompany him to a meeting, which several of the farmers had called to address a number of the issues at stake. I had agreed, intrigued, completely forgetting that James now headed the giant multi-company organisation that bought and milled the cane we grew. I took extra care to dress in a smart black number. I knew half of the Mount Edgecombe community would be there and, since my parents were still leading social figures, I didn't feel like letting the Whitney side of things down.

I must say there was a stir as we arrived, Kicker leaning on my arm, as he proceeded to his accustomed place at the vast mahogany board table. Women in the boardroom! What was Mount Edgecombe coming to! I enjoyed the sensation. It had been such a long time since I had been conscious of turning a few heads.

"Well, Joss, how are you?" Those well remembered tones... the voice within the memoirs of my heart.

"James," I said, by way of acknowledgement.

"McKelvey! Still robbing us farmers of an honest living, eh?" As usual, Kicker was direct to a fault. James merely smiled. He expected no less from the old man and was not fazed by his needling at all.

"Well, Mr Whitney, I see you've brought reinforcements this time," James replied, smiling again and nodding in my direction. He was quite grey at the temples. The sun had left deep creases at the edges of his brown eyes, dark, direct as ever.

There was not much I could contribute to the meeting. I was still learning the ropes with regard to those aspects of cane production; nevertheless I felt I had acquitted myself reasonably well. I could see that James was impressed that I had a grasp of the detail involved. I felt ridiculously pleased when he took my hand and said, "We'll see you at the next meeting, no doubt."

"Yes, indeed," I replied.

"What about a hack one of these weekends? We could ride over to Jameson's farm across the ridge one Saturday?"

"I'd like that, James. It'd be like the old days."

"Perhaps you could bring a companion? Kerry doesn't ride much."

"Yes, that would be nice. But companions are difficult these days, especially ones who ride… especially at our age..." He laughed.

"You're a beautiful woman, Joss," he said. And then it was over, and Kicker and I were on our way home.

In the silence as I drove, Kicker suddenly said, "Not a bad young CEO, James McKelvey. Knows his sugar." I listened, surprised. "Pity about that bastard Edward, though. Never could see eye to eye with him. Always buggered everything up wherever he was."

"Why, Dad? Why do you say that?" I asked, after a pause. Kicker looked reflective.

"Someday, Jossie, you're going to have to sit down and have a long discussion with your mother and sort all this rubbish out. No good talking to me. I hate the buggers. All of them."

"Why, Dad," I asked again. "Why don't you talk about them? What happened, Dad… between you and Edward McKelvey?"

"Talk to your mother, Joss," Kicker said roughly, and then fell silent. Pretty soon he had nodded off. I had to wake him to help him to the veranda when we arrived home.

"A penny for those thoughts of yours, Joss,"

my mother said. A sudden vision of her and Edward rose to my mind. I shook my head, and saw the familiar look of concern. She put her hand on my arm and settled herself in the chair next to mine. I did not want to tell her what Kicker had said. Lying there, crystal glass in hand, concealed in the familiar hollow of cushion and cane on the veranda, my waiting place, I could hear the usual musical notes of tree frogs heralding the night as they clung to the fig tree. Long since habituated to the demanding life of cane farming, the hours in the saddle, the protracted nights of accounts and figures, I was more concerned with my growing isolation and emptiness, than any bodily fatigue I may have been experiencing. The sugar plantation was an intense involvement eagerly sought, for just such moments of pleasant weariness, to lie strewn across the veranda chair watching the unfolding drama of the Mount Edgecombe skies. This chair had held my mother each evening for so long, and now held me. We had both waited here. But it was no longer enough, this waiting... this endless waiting. Why was I so restless?

Reflecting on Kicker's earlier words, I became aware that the ancient curse on our family had become a familiar. The thing that had mattered so much, the thing that had destroyed us and pulled apart, had dissipated into the mould of age, rubbed down by time, robbed of malevolence, as it turned fainter and fainter in our memories. Suddenly I felt it was time to throw off past wrongs. I wanted release from all this waiting...a renaissance. I was tired of being on my own, apart and withdrawn. I felt I could be a friend to James. We needed to be friends. It would be easier for Kerry and me. I had released James to Kerry long ago, surely? Yes, it would be good to give my life some better meaning than an obsession with Heritage and its production of cane, its wonderful skies and long busy days. In my heart of hearts, I began to look forward to the seeing James.

"You look a little happier, Jossie. Are you sure you're not pining, darling?"

"Ah, no, Ma. Don't worry. It's fine. Honestly. Isn't the sky great this evening?"

It was to be a long while, Anna, before I was to have the conversation with my mother that I really wanted, the one that would resolve the central doubts and innermost questions of my life and bring my persistently shifting thoughts to rest. There was a great deal of heartache to go before that... Many things had yet to transpire before that singular event that had separated the McKelveys and the Whitneys... whatever it was... found a satisfactory conclusion. This event, concealed, buried away, never mentioned... this is what had driven the wedge between our parents and had taken James from me. Why could they not tell me? Neither my mother nor my father could tell me... So I returned to my waiting place and threw myself into figures and production and disputes again, returned to hard riding, long gallops along the edges of the cane, with my horse thundering below me, urging him on recklessly, glad to be caught up in the concentration of controlling him, so I would not lose my balance and die in the flying of the hooves.

CHAPTER FIFTEEN

One evening, Krivahnen summoned me to the telephone, rolling his eyes and grinning approval from ear to ear.

"It's a gentleman, Miss. And he is asking after you. Will you be taking the call?" I nodded, kicked off my riding boots and settled myself comfortably before putting the receiver to my ear.

"Joss, it's me. Riaan. How are you?" I hardly recognised his voice, after all that time.

"Oh... hello... how are you, Riaan?" Krivahnen busied himself with laying out a drinks tray, fiddling with the ice cubes and refolding the linen napkin several times.

"I've been wondering lately about you, Joss. I saw you at the meet the other day but I couldn't get your attention. The crowd was too big. I saw your daughter too." My heart gave a lurch. "She's grown up now, hey? How are you getting on? How are you, really?"

"No, fine."

"Ja, I've sort of been keeping track of you,

Jossie… from time to time. Helen Denton gave me your number. Hope you don't mind… it's okay if I phone?"

"It's nice to hear from you, Riaan. How are things?" Krivahnen positively beamed at me.

"No, ja, fine. The school's still there. I'm the deputy, now. Keeps me busy. But tell me, how are things with you? It must be all of fifteen years now, hey, Joss?"

"Something like that, Riaan. Something like that." Krivahnen actually bounced out with a spring in his step the moment he heard me accepting Riaan's suggestion that we had a drink together. I heard him say to my mother, whom he surprised in the passage, "Oh my, Ma'am. Miss Jossie will be having a date, pretty soon. This gentleman Riaan will be taking her, and all. Oh, Ma'am, may the gods be praised, indeed. After all, it is for too long she has been sitting in the desert of widowhood and wasting, as it is said, like the many a flower that blooms unseen. All these long years only her all alone. Oh my, Ma'am, is it not too wonderful, indeed!" My heart went out to him, faithful old retainer that he was, although I did not particularly enjoy being the subject of everyone's conversation in these matters. First Kerry, now Krivahnen, in on the act.

I realised I was looking forward to anything that would add a change of pace to my life. The long evenings alone on the veranda were getting to me. The years had been far too long.

However, I must say I was nervous when Riaan arrived. He had not changed much. He was grey now, his hair receding, much heavier than I remembered. He walked directly into the lounge and took my hand.

"Jossie! *Liefling*. You look wonderful. You don't look like the mother of a teenager… you look like … like you always did. A bit thinner though." He smiled with the warm direct openness I remembered of him.

"Would you like to meet her, Riaan?" I wanted to get things over with. "Come in, Anna, darling. Come and meet Riaan Berkhout."

You stepped shyly from the doorway where you had been waiting, Anna. Riaan, used to adolescents, bowed slightly and lifted his hand to greet you but I saw that he was held in a subtle web of tension. Riaan had discovered something. He was here to find out about it. I could see it in the sweep of his eyes as he looked at you.

"May I introduce you to my daughter, Anna? Say hello to Mr Berkhout, Anna." Riaan drew in an audible breath, as he caught closer sight of your face. He brought up his hand once more to shake yours, just managing to take in my unmasked look of appeal.

"Good God, Joss. She looks just like you," he said, his revelation emerging clearly in his tone. He continued to chat easily and naturally to you, Anna, making you laugh, glad of something to keep himself talking, until I sent you off to so that we could leave.

Riaan was quiet as we drove to the club. Twice we tried to say something simultaneously, laughing awkwardly at the other's interruption. However, Riaan was always easy to be with and, within a drink or two, I found myself relaxing in his company, and even enjoying the dance we had, while he asked me a flurry of questions, avoiding his new and sudden discovery, but intent on getting me to enjoy myself. Once or twice he fell silent and shook his head slightly as though coming to terms with things. I liked the comfortable way he held me on the dance floor. It was good to be dancing again. It was fine to be held against the muscle and bone of a man, and my body responded instinctively and subtly to his appreciation. During the course of the evening, he held my arm up and wordlessly traced the pale scars on my wrists with his fingers. It was such an intimate and gentle thing.

"Jossie! Well, fancy finding you here! What a dark horse, you are!" Kerry, with James at her elbow, approached us. "I've been trying for years to hitch you up with one of the Mount Edgecombe availables, sorry lot that they are, and here you are dancing with the most attractive man in the room! Well done."

Sometimes Kerry was a lot like her mother. I did not look at James. Nothing ever seemed to alter my ridiculous reaction to James's proximity. My mother's masks and my Wykeford training rescued me immediately.

"Can I introduce you to Riaan Berkhout? Riaan, James and Kerry McKelvey." Soon the men were involved in animated conversation. James obviously liked Riaan.

"Well, Joss. Riaan says he is a most willing companion to you for that ride we've often spoken about and never done. How about next Saturday? Kerry, can you put together a picnic and stay with the old folk while we go out? We can take the youngsters with us." She nodded enthusiastically.

"That's wonderful, Joss. We'd be *very* happy to have Riaan stay over, wouldn't we, James? It's too far to go all the way back to Kloof after a full ride like that." Shades of Aunt Millie! Kerry was positively winking approval and support in my direction. All she needed was the hair net.

"Joss, you sly thing," she said as they left,

and I had to laugh. Kerry was such a good friend.

I invited Riaan in for coffee and we chatted on in the bonhomie generated by the evening. He was an engaging man, and I found myself wondering why he had not found someone else in the years that had intervened. Riaan did not try to kiss me that evening. He waited until day of the picnic for that. I could have foreseen that happening. What he did say, however, as he left, was, "We'll have to do some talking *this* time, *liefling*. We'll have to talk about everything soon... *né?*"

The day of the picnic, as I recall it, was one of those halcyon days, fresh and fair, perfect weather rising up from the south and spreading across Mount Edgecombe like a cerulean sari shot through with patterns of diaphanous light.

"Does Anna ride too?" asked Riaan when he arrived at Heritage soon after sunrise.

"Probably as well as you, if not better.

"Chip off the old block, hey, *liefling?*"

"Which block, Riaan?" I said as evenly as I could, pouring him a cup of coffee. My hand was perfectly steady. Just then, you came through on to the veranda, in boots and jodhpurs, riding crop. You had been up since first light, waking up the grooms a good half hour before that was really necessary.

"Shall I bring the horses up, Mum?" When I nodded, you flew off to the stables.

"Let's discuss that later, *liefling*. We need to, né?" Riaan said, very seriously. "You should have told me, Joss."

Striding across the lawns to where you held our horses, Anna, I wondered what possessed me to readmit Riaan into my life. I would have to take the greatest care. His feelings for me had apparently changed little. People are generally constant in the affairs of the heart. I know that. You love only once. Everything else is a rehearsal or an encore.

He was quite taken with you, Anna, helping you up to your saddle, tightening the girth, checking the length of your stirrup leathers. He has an easy way with people, your father.

Suddenly I felt I had to stop living for myself in the vast interiors of my own guilt and confusion. I had to give him back to you. I did not want you living the circumstances of your life, forever not knowing, forever uncertain, as circumstances had forced me to. I did not want you to become like me, or my mother. I resolved to let things develop as they would. Whatever other consequences came about, however afraid I was of them, you needed your father. However, on that wonderful, fresh Mount Edgecombe morning, you were still too young, I considered, to bear such knowledge yet. Riaan would have to wait until you and I were both ready, before I was going to allow him to reveal his relationship to anybody.

We flew along the gravel, leather creaking, and the chinking of bits and irons forming a refrain for the drumming hooves of our horses. Riaan watched, already growing in fatherly concern, as you pulled away in your usual wild jockey gallop. I hoped Riaan was going to be sensible about you, my beautiful wild independent fifteen-year-old, my daughter without knowledge fatherly things. I was glad of the focus required to spur our horses on, driving through the cane fields, to catch up with your careless, confident mastery, your rising up to meet the dongas and the fences between us.

Exhilarated, we flew through the fresh morning, astride flowing, shining, moving muscle. Above, fish eagles wheeled and our hard breathing and the snorting of the horses merged in a high song with their fluted calls. Around us, the fields swirled in silvered dancing sheen, rustling in harmony, an opus of sound and movement. We galloped on to meet the McKelveys, taking fence after fence, thundering along the firebreaks, churning up soot and soil, clearing *vlei* after *vlei*. Finally we pulled up, breathlessly laughing and shouting to one another.

"When's Dean getting here, Mama? Why are they taking so long? Where are they?"

"Tie up the horses, Anna. Don't be so impatient... and, Anna, next time you take fences like that, and make me do it too, I'm going to have more than just a few words with you. Take care of your horse, even if you don't care what happens to you, young lady!" You remained quite unconcerned, and moved off to loosen girdles and rub muzzles, feeling for sugar cubes in your back pocket.

"She's lovely, Joss," said Riaan. I acknowledged this by looking directly into his eyes. "Now tell me why you didn't say anything to me?" he continued. Colour must have flooded my face because he said, more gently, " These years must have been hard for you..."

"I... I just need a little time to get it right with her, Riaan. She's young yet... too young. She's not ready..."

Riaan paused for several moments. "And you, *liefling*, are you ready? She won't be, unless you are," he said slowly. Car hooters announcing the arrival of Kerry and the elder McKelveys interrupted further conversation.

"Where's Dean?" You came running up, and tugged at Kerry's arm.

"He's coming, Anna," she said smiling. "They

had a bit of trouble with a cast shoe. They'll be along directly Blackwell has replaced it." Kerry helped Sarah McKelvey, now frail from a wasting sickness, to settle comfortably in a deck chair, while Edward and I spread blankets and unpacked hampers in anticipation of a long day of fresh air and conviviality. Edward was still lithe and strong, comfortable with his retirement, and gallantly courteous towards me, protective almost, despite my slight awkwardness with a man I did not know well at all and with whom I had had no more than a dozen words of conversation in my life.

I could not help noticing that Kerry had marks of fatigue beneath her eyes and fine strained lines in her face.

"You okay, Ker?" I asked.

"Mmm. I seem to be coming down with something. I get so exhausted these days. I'll have to check it out with old Doc Moffat." She smiled, pushing back a strand of hair from her face. My anxiety lessened. Little did I know how very concerned about her we were all to become. She placed her hand on my arm.

Kerry began rummaging in the picnic baskets. "You're a good friend, Joss," she suddenly. I nodded. "Where did you find that man? You seem to have known each other for ages?" she continued. I nodded again, wondering if in any way she was referring to a resemblance, slight though it was, between you and Riaan.

"He was teaching at the school when I was there, Kerry. He's one of the deputies now. You met him once at Peter's funeral."

Never explain and don't complain, I thought to myself.

"O ho, Joss, the plot thickens. That's more than fifteen years ago. How long have you been seeing him, hmm?" There was no doubt about it. Kerry was Aunt Milly's daughter through and through.

"Cut it out, you," I said uncomfortably, handing on picnic equipment for her to set up.

"Really, though, Joss, I'm so pleased for you. Remember how I was just saying the other day you need a bit of company. It's so boring when you don't come to the club because you don't want to be on your own. I'm looking forward to us being a foursome. What about it, hey? James likes him a lot... Talking about couples, what do you think of old Beau making an honest woman of my mother at long last? What an on-off wedding that one has become."

"That's right! You told me. When is the wedding?"

Kerry began slicing sandwiches.

"The wedding? Oh, at Christmas. They're getting married at the registry office, thank God! My mum wanted to organise a whole white wedding church thing, but I think even she realised that old Beau's past standing up for longer than a few minutes at a time these days... Quite sweet really, wanting to get married at their age... Can't imagine what for... Anyway, I'm looking forward to seeing you at the reception with your new man, nogal."

She paused briefly, looking around for the teenagers, waving a plate of sandwiches at them. "Do you think your mum and Kicker will come? Even with Edward and Sarah there. That lot seemed to have mellowed in their dotage, the old ones... all of them. I guess it takes energy to feud and witter when you're getting on like they are. Sarah never says anything about you lot. Neither does Edward. He gets quite agitated if I chat about you. I never understood why none of them got on. Did you?"

At that point Dean and James arrived at a sedate trot. They had obviously been chatting to each other with pleasure along the way. Kerry looked up at James, smiling. I saw suddenly the same helpless loving look that had brought my tango to a halt on the night of my engagement to Peter. That look had appeared so often in my restless puzzled dreams through the years, I knew it intimately. James dropped from his saddle, handing his reins to Dean, and kissed Kerry with the carelessness and comfort of long years of marriage. He greeted his parents, taking a little extra time with Sarah and shaking hands with Riaan.

"I'm so glad you came, Titch," he said to me. I could do nothing about the stupid vaulting of my heart. Oh thank God for Wykeford, for my mother's masks, for my years of training. I would rather have been immolated on a widow's pyre than let Kerry, or James, or anyone, become aware of James's effect on me. And so I was able to turn to Kerry and say quite naturally, "Have we finished, Ker?"

He had called me Titch.

"Well get off on that hack of yours, the lot of you," said Kerry. "Sarah and I will lie under the shade and do sensible things. Dad will look after us, not so? What about a glass of plonk here, Dad? Dean, make sure you take care of Anna, now," Kerry tucked her hand through Edward McKelvey's arm. I'll always remember how the sunlight flicked behind her. The McKelveys doted on her. All four of them. She was a central point and they revolved around her merry and relaxed being, balanced just because she was there. I could never have been that to them.

"Come, *liefling*, up you go." Riaan gave me a lift into the saddle and I powered away along the *vlei*, riding the mare as hard as I could. She flew across the ploughed soil, sucking in the wind through distended nostrils, the silk of her chestnut mane flying in my face. Looking back over my shoulder, I saw Riaan break away on his borrowed mount to catch up with me, James holding back to stay with Anna and Dean. I felt confused and angry and berated myself for my own endless nonsense about James. We must have ridden for a good half-hour like that. I easily held my lead on Riaan. I knew this land, its contours and ridges, its sharp breaking away from hills into valleys and up again and I knew my horse. I knew what she could do. Feeling her tiring beneath me, I reined her in and sat waiting in the saddle for Riaan.

"Great Heavens, Joss! What a pace," he called breathlessly. He pulled up alongside of me. "You've got the advantage here," he continued ruefully, "but wait until we're on home ground. Unfair advantage, *liefie*. Man, I couldn't get near you." I liked the way he said "kooden" with that Afrikaans burr of his. He dropped to the ground beside me, looping his reins through the crook of his arm, and reached up to help me down, taking my waist in his hands.

"Johanna," he said over my shoulder and, as I turned to face him, he put his arms around me and kissed me intensely, hungrily. "She's mine, isn't she?" he said against my ear. "And you too, *liefling*, you too. Jy is myne."

"Riaan, I..." But he kissed me again, covering the words with his mouth, there between the horses as they nuzzled grass at our feet.

"Your mom's got a boyfriend!" I heard Dean floating through the air, teasing you. "Your mom's got a boyfriend... Your mom's... Ouch," as you gave him a good slap. I looked up at James, my face aflame. He dismounted, smiled at me, and said to Riaan, "About time someone takes care of her. About time." I mounted my mare hurriedly. Oh Anna, I still see the two of them standing there. They're smiling broadly in the dust and the drifting sunlight...

"You men! You think you know everything," I say and take off down the road, hiding confusion, fighting chagrin and irritation, trying to work out the inevitabilities my situation seems, eternally, to demand of me.

And so it was that your father and I fell into our companionship. Riaan always said he was a patient man. And he was. You seemed so precious a gift to him that he would rein himself in to any extent, not to disturb the precarious balance between us. I have always enjoyed his company. He's a cultured, exceptional being, your father, Anna. You easily grew to love him, as you should. No one could have a better father... or a dearer, finer friend... but I run on...

Much was yet to happen before I discovered his true merit as a fine man, his sheer integrity and his personal grace. There are so many things I still have to tell you, Anna. Your father, Riaan, did not only receive, but, also, *returned* my life's most treasured gift to me. Let me tell you how. But first, I must say how we got to that point. What a long story you have asked for, Anna!

CHAPTER SIXTEEN

Not long after that picnic, we were saddened to hear that Sarah McKelvey had died in her sleep. James and Kerry, Milly, Edward, Kicker, and my mother, Johanna Nel Whitney... we were all affected by Sarah's passing in one way or another.

Kerry appeared to be most particularly affected. When I tried to comfort her, I ascertained for the first time that Kerry had formed an alliance with her mother-in-law that had served to carry her through her own long years of loving James.

"She's gone, Joss... She's gone. She is... was... a real example to me. She knew what it's like... these McKelvey men..." Kerry looked up at me, saw my face. "You think it's easy being with James, Joss? Oh, James has been kind, so loving, good father, good husband - but I wish he would *love* me. I want him to love me!" Kerry was wrapped in her grief.

"Oh Ker..." I said helplessly. "Oh, Ker."

"Everything is correct with him, he does everything the right... but, there's something in him, Joss, something he holds back. It's been like that from the beginning... it's like a shadow between us." I bit my lip and looked down at Kerry's hands, as she twisted a handkerchief through her fingers. "He's never given me the best part of himself," she said miserably. I put my hand up, trying to find the right words.

"Sarah knew that. She knew that," Kerry cried out.

Kerry would never know how deeply her heartrending cry had found its mark. I had always considered Kerry to be basically an inoffensive unaffected carbon copy of Auntie Milly, with slightly more substance and much more grace. Until that moment I had not recognised that Sarah must have known better than most how it was for Kerry loving James as she did. Sarah and my mother had a knowledge that Kerry also shared, for all their distance. Sarah *knew* Kerry, *knew* my mother. And I knew Kerry. I felt the deepest shame well up within me. I sat mutely trying to find a way to comfort her, trying to be the friend she had unfailingly been to me, trying to listen to her sorrow, conscious of my protracted, graceless self-involvement through the years. I had never thought that she, like all of us, had to struggle with the submerged parts of herself, while the sunny tip of her thrust itself up into that light of observation and inference which fools us into thinking we know each other well. It was awful to find I was less than Kerry thought of me.

Life has such a way of turning screws most precisely and intensely so that it can catch us in its movements. We're ground and ground until we pay the price of our dues. Before another year passed, there was to be one more dying, a loss which brought all of us back to the graveside, shocked, grieving... mourning a departure which was beyond all reasoning.

But not before Aunt Millicent finally hooked her man.

CHAPTER SEVENTEEN

Oh, I do remember Milly's wedding well. Yes, Uncle Beau and Auntie Milly had a wonderful wedding! My mother was delighted at the opportunity to organise one of her famous events, and pulled out all the stops. It was not the majestic occasion of years past. Things were no longer done in such grand style, but the small reception was impeccably and stylishly arranged, as ever.

In the afternoon hours before the ceremony, I was drawn to reminiscences of the day before my own marriage to Peter Carney. My mother, Kerry and I plied Auntie Milly with far too many celebratory drinks as we got her dressed and ready. The nervous bride was only too pleased to soothe her fluttering nerves with a number of stiff whisky shots.

However, I did have the opportunity, before things got a little out of hand, to draw Auntie Milly aside and thank her for the many times she had stood by me and cared for me. I was surprised when tears filled her eyes and she grasped my hands.

"That's all right, lovie, you always were my favourite thing." She gave me a hug. She had become spindly with age. She felt thin and insubstantial.

"I'm so glad you finally got your man, Milly," I said, hugging her back.

"Time you got one of your own, Jossie," she said gruffly, and gave me another squeeze. I became aware, suddenly, of all the years she had been on her own.

"It's taken Uncle Beau a long time to get around to this, hasn't it?" I asked.

"Thirty five years, if you have to know. It's ridiculous, Joss... Don't *you* leave everything until there's nothing left... hee, hee... if you know what I mean! Beau is a bit overdue with just about everything, hey, my dearie? If he hadn't popped the question soon, we'd probably be laying out for the final journey instead of the trip down the aisle, if you know what I mean. But he's stood by, you know. Stood by so nicely." She gave a little screech of laughter and swigged another shot from her glass. "It's not good, Joss, being on your own, and it's not as if *you* don't have choices. You're not an old mattress like me. Don't waste the years, my darling. Don't waste them."

"Ah, Auntie Milly, you enjoy it now. It's your day, and it's a lovely one for a wedding."

She smiled.

"Yes, it is, isn't it, my lovie?" she said smugly.

I don't know what possessed my mother, and Auntie Milly come to think of it, to allow me to persuade them to imbibe at the rate they did on that day, of all days. Occasionally, my well-mannered, socially graceful mother was capable of falling off the wagon, but hardly in this spectacular way. However, she and Auntie Milly outdid themselves all afternoon. They drank whisky, copiously. Weddings seemed to bring this kind of behaviour out in them.

"Didn't you say you and Uncle Beau had been engaged once?" I asked.

"Dearie me, that's a long story that one," Milly giggled. My mother looked uncomfortable.

"This isn't the time to tell it, Millicent," she said.

"But I will. Hanna, I want to. Wha's the harm now? These things are all gone and forgotten after all, f'rgiven an' f'rgotten, and there you have it, hey?" My mother looked at her, realising she was determined, in her cups, to have her say. She faced Milly squarely.

"*I* will tell the girls, Milly." My mother's slurred enunciation sounded little better than Milly's. The whisky was beginning to tell on her too. "Well, after these two were first engaged, Uncle Beau misbehaved himself, and Auntie Milly found him trying to kiss me." At this, Milly gave a gentle sob. "Oh, Milly stop your nonsense. He was drunk, the stupid fool..."

"Don't call my Beau a fool, Johanna," Milly interrupted snappily, before taking another long sip at her glass, and subsiding on the sofa, blinking and patting her eyes with a tissue.

"He is, Milly... a complete dolt." My mother's

words jerked Milly into a few more passing moments of sobriety. "Milly wouldn't listen to anyone," my mother continued, ignoring Milly's protest. "She just went off and found someone else to marry... your father, Kerry... and left us all trying to pacify an unpacifiable Beau for the next few decades. That's the reason I say he's such a complete idiot... it's taken him thirty five damn years to convince Milly it was quite different from what she thought. You know, Milly, in your day, it was quite easy to mistake the two of us for each other. We were so alike... still are... He thought he was kissing *you*." My mother pointed her glass in Milly's general direction.

"No, he didn't," rejoined Milly mournfully. I'm ashamed to say that Kerry and I fell about laughing. My mother and Millicent formed such a contrast - in everything. The thought of them being alike in anything was too funny for words!

"But we made up quickly, didn't we, Jo?" said Milly went on rather stupidly.

"Oh yes, dear heart. Oh yes, of course we

did. Best friends, haven't we always been, Mill? You've seen me through some times." My mother came to a halt, and I saw gratitude in some of the hurt her memories had suddenly brought. She took Milly's hand in hers. "Millicent... no one has been a dearer, truer friend."

"I know, Jo," said Auntie Milly, perfectly soberly. "I know." My mother put her arms round the uncertain old lady.

In that gesture, I gained some idea of the things my mother had had to share with Auntie Milly through the years. My mother was lucky. I realised suddenly how much Auntie Milly had been a constant for me too, stalwart and dear. And Kerry was the same - my friend unfaltering, and so cherished by me, especially now.

"He should have done this years ago, Mill, years ago... the dolt!" said my mother fiercely, as they held on to each other.

By the time Uncle Beau arrived to bear his bride off to the magistrate's court, Milly was well and truly merry. She did not have the full benefit of Beau's long and familiar acquaintance with alcohol, nor his ability to stay on his feet. However, like him, she had lost the ability to maintain full control of his tongue under such circumstances.

"Well, m'dear. Bit under the weather, wot? Eh?" Beau said when he saw her weaving backwards and forwards in an attempt to kiss him hello. Milly smile, somewhat unfocusedly at her husband to be and hiccoughed loudly. He rocked from side to side, his head weaving in unison with Auntie Millie, lips pursed, endeavouring to plant a kiss on her face in return.

"Good God, woman, keep still, won't you. It's like trying to kiss a cobra."

"Parron," she said. "Hanna says I must kiss you, Beau. Le' me kiss you, you fool."

"Bit nervous, are we, ol' gel? Never fear, m'dear, ol' Beau's right here. A strong arm here. Can lean on it, wot, eh? Stop staggering around, female. Take a hold of me arm!" Milly smiled brightly up at him and settled her dishevelled hat at a more rakish angle to allow its net to drape across her face. She hiccoughed again.

"Come on, ol' gel," Beau said gently, "Get under sail. Can't be letting the old side down. Best foot for'ud, m'gel. Must stand upright at the hitching post. Come on, old thing. Best foot, wot? Best foot." Milly continued to cling unsteadily to his arm.

"Oh Beau, dear, we're getting married in the morning. Ding dong. Ding dong."

"Give a hand here, old cock." This said by Beau to Krivahnen, who bustled about, helping herd the reluctant bride into the wedding vehicle.

"Madam, you'll be creasing your somewhat beautiful wedding dress, and all," said Krivahnen, as he gently ushered her forward. "You'll be getting into the bridal conveyance now, will you, madam, in order not to be late for the matrimonial ceremony, yes?" Milly patted him on the head and placidly got into the car. Krivahnen had a wonderful way with children and old people. She waved gaily from the back window as the car proceeded down the driveway.

"Mum," I said severely, "What possessed the two of you to drink so much?"

"You, Joss. You and memories, Joss. We were just laying some ghosts. Putting a few things behind us. We go back a long way, dearest." These words gave me cause to reflect further. Hanna Whitney and Milly D'Unienville. Kerry McKelvey and Joss Carney. I had a sudden vision of Kerry and myself, a decade or two on, leaning comfortably together in friendship, weathered by the years into understanding, holding on to each other when we could not hold on anywhere else. Perhaps we'd also be drinking just a few too many, as we faced the new and uncertain experiences of handing Dean and you on to someone in marriage. I was struck by a sudden thought. Heartache. Just heartache. Oh God, as long as I didn't have to hand you on to Dean. Such ambiguity to be a mother, such a facing up to the knowledge that love was going to extract its dues.

At the magistrate's office, Auntie Milly acquitted herself reasonably well, despite one or two unsteady attempts to mount the stairs. I heard the magistrate say to his clerk, *sotto voce*, on becoming aware of the odour of whisky trailing not only the bride, but the groom also, to whom, of course, the reek was an habitual cologne, "Better not light a cigarette here. We'll all be blown to Kingdom come!" This caused my mother to giggle inappropriately and the ceremony became less serious than it might have been. Kicker heartily enjoyed my mother's rare moments of silliness, and egged her on. Her shoulders shook with suppressed mirth at his running comments. He also clapped Beau heartily on the back when the groom's attention drifted from the magistrate and fixed upon his weaving bride for too long. But he was, as ever, incredibly gentle with Milly, always leaving her person out of his sly Irish taunts and ribald mocking. There was so much I did not know about my parents. What had brought about this event, this marriage, these particular interactions of friendship? Weren't life's endlessly repeating patterns just so strange?

When Beau and Milly turned, as man and wife, to walk between us they were unexpectedly transformed. They smiled, as all couples do, transported with the joy of marriage's first few moments. He was proud of her. This old degenerate was bursting with pride and joy, his chest puffed out and his arm held snappily up for her to lean on. And she looked as if she could not believe her luck. She was dazed with happiness, with relief, with absolute, unashamed love. No matter that it had taken the best part of half a century to get to this point. It had now arrived.

"I wish you well, Auntie Milly," I murmured, as I gave them a hug, and then I joined the others to shower them with handfuls of confetti.

Kicker and my mother were holding hands. My mother looked as if his broad arm had moulded her, as she leant against him. How faithful my parents had been to each other through the long years behind them. How utterly supportive of one another, no matter what. A bewildering stab of loneliness ran through me. I envied them. I envied my mother and Kicker, their being there with one other, come what may - their staying power, their longevity - in the face of the things that had been.

Behind the bridal pair, whose descent of the stairs was steadier than the ascent of them, after my mother and Kicker, came the elder McKelvey, Edward, straight-backed, his eyes on my mother, alone, no longer with Sarah beside him. Then James and Kerry and Dean, and after that, you and I, Anna... yes, and Riaan... in procession, playing our roles in the confluence of things. We all had a good time at Auntie Milly's wedding.

CHAPTER EIGHTEEN

The memories flood in now. Mostly they blur into each other in patterns of joy and guilt, loss and gain, reflecting the hues of any ordinary life... ah, but which life is ordinary, Anna? This is the way the clock ticks within us, the passing moments gathered inexorably, with or without our consent. Time passes. Things happen. We weave meanings from that blur. Sometimes the shapes don't fit. However hard we try, they just don't piece themselves together. Nevertheless, we are together here, Anna. We sit in this room on the eve of your wedding and we stitch and tuck and join this dress of satin and lace, and you sit listening intently to me, knowing this is the gift you asked of me. As if this explanation, this act of contrition for only being able to be what I am and to do what I am able to is any gift indeed!

Kerry was my good friend, darling. I had to learn to lose her long before she went, not abruptly like Peter, but in weeks and months and increments. And, afterwards, by having to learn to let her leave us, save for questioning the designs of reason, the begging of God to supply the purpose in such a senseless departure. Her going was measured intensely in an ebb and flow of despair and hope, in rare courage and in endurance, before we all, finally, allowed her to slip away.

Soon after Auntie Milly and Beau got married, Kerry persuaded me to join her on holiday. "Come on, Jossie. It'll be such fun. James had built on to the cottage, and there's a lovely bedroom for you and Riaan. Port Edward's just a couple of hours away and surely Kicker can do without you for a couple of weeks? Come, Joss, you and Riaan, hey? And the kids. Dean doesn't want to go without Anna. Come on, Joss. Do it." So, I reflected ruefully, everyone's made Riaan a permanent feature in my life. Well, if Mount Edgecombe society had decreed it, who was I to argue, and if friends and family thought so too, it had to be fairly inevitable.

If there was any awkwardness about the

arrangements, it was between Riaan and me when the assumptions about our relationship took the form of being assigned, quite matter of factly, to the same bedroom. These concerns made a useful shield to other unbidden thoughts. Dear God, would I never let the man go and just take what I could from the here-and-now realities left to me! I thought that I had long since mastered my stubborn psyche through heartfelt friendship with Kerry and a deep respect for James, and in the comfort of Riaan's companionship.

It was fine to have Riaan there at the McKelvey beach cottage. James sat with his arm around Kerry, beer in hand, chatting comfortably with Riaan. Kerry seemed unusually quiet, but quite happy to lie against James's shoulder listening to him talking. The four of us began to relax with each other, sitting on the postage stamp veranda, watching the sun's falling into a shifting sea. Even the stars, seeming to fall into eternity despite their shimmering primordial patterns, flooded the sea into fracture. Ah, I remember the sound of the sea as it sucked at the dunes and the rocks and spat back at us with its ancient sandy sounds, which prompted us to walk our separate ways. James and Kerry. Me and Riaan.

Sometimes, just sometimes, our hearts beat in unison in a perfect echo of the rhythms of the universe. I can still feel the air against my nostrils, reeking of herb and weed, and the taste of fish in my mouth, and the texture of the sand beneath me, the feel of your father's hand on my breast, his mouth feeding me kisses that came unexpectedly and suddenly. It is a night forever impressed in me, coherently recalled, and perfectly remembered. I will not forget it... or the event that followed.

Your father and I stayed out a long time, and then sauntered back arm in arm, dazzled and dreamy, overwhelmed by resplendent passing moments. When he fell asleep beside me, and I lay turning my face from one side of the pillow to the other trying to work it all out, the sound of a raw cry, bled from anguish, brought me to my feet and running to Kerry's door.

It was James. James had cried out.

Suspended at the door, my heart beating with presentiment, I heard him saying, "Darling... darling, it's all right. We can get through this thing, we can..." His voice cracked with agony. "Oh Kerry, Kerry, darling..." The words Kerry uttered next sent me straight back to your father to lie silent and awake beside him until a merciful dawn let its light in through the window. She said, "I'm sorry James. I didn't mean to upset you. I'm so scared, James. I'm so scared of dying."

I waited until James and Riaan had gone off with Dean and Anna, and we were sitting together shelling peas for supper the next day.

"What's going on, Kerry? Tell me why you're looking so tired and distraught. What's wrong with you?" I don't think I ever admired Kerry's courage more than when she said, pulling herself together so straight forwardly, her eyes holding the appeal that she did not have the courage for this, "I had these tests. They're all positive. It's cancer and it's is pretty far advanced."

"Oh dear God, Kerry. Oh my God!" I could not help this crying out.

"I can handle this Joss. I can." She grasped my hand in her own. She was trembling.

"Well, you're not going to handle it on your own," I said fiercely, raging within me, raging at the stupid wanton destruction that had suddenly blossomed like a dark flower amongst us. And all the while I had not know, was not aware of, the things she had been carrying with her on this most singular of journeys. "You're not on your own on this one, Kerry. James and Riaan, my parents and Edward, all of us... we're right there behind you, don't you worry. And you are going to fight it, Kerry. You are going to beat it." How inadequate I must have sounded! I held her head against my shoulder and rocked her, and raged at the clodhopping stupidity of destiny, the idiocy of fate. Kerry was not quite forty-four. She was not going to die. I was going to make sure of that. James was going to. We would love her enough, hold her enough. We would *make* her better.

But death is a more powerful adversary than anger, Anna. The melanomas forced us to watch her slip away, each day a little less of her, each week a bit more pain. She became determined to live, and we were just as determined that she was going to, not knowing then what this kind of struggle can cost.

Memories of my conversations with her at this time still serrate my mind. They keep me awake in the dark hours. "I can't lie down any more, Joss. I can't get comfortable. I have to sit all the time. Talk to me, Jossie, talk to me, please," and later, "The pain won't go anymore. Help me bear it, Jossie. Help me." Then, throat eaten away, breath gone, "Tell me about James again, Jossie. How you used to look for mongoose eggs beneath your house, and what he used to say to you," and later still and small and motionless like a tree frog, "What will Dean do without me?" And finally, "I don't want them to see me like this, Joss. I don't want to put them through this. Look what's left of me. Tell them to stay away. Tell them to give me something to end this, please, Jossie, please. Get something for me. Help me end it. Help me."

In God's love, how can anyone be put through such a suffering? How can anyone, *anyone*, endure such terrible degradation! Oh Anna, she fell away like that, beyond us, out of reach of our grasping hearts, away from life, crucified beyond morphine, tortured past all possible reasoning! I begged, I prayed, I bargained. Over and over again, I tried to accept, yet flesh and bone continued to fall away, until only the raw courage remained. Oh brave and loving friend... my friend of grace and pain. I miss her! I miss her so much.

James used to sit with her, hour after hour, his thumb gently rubbing the back of her wasted hand, talking of current things, future things, coaxing her when she would not eat, making her part of the ordinary things she missed so much. I knew the passing days were stripping him too and bleakness gathered round him when he stepped from her room to stand at the end of the veranda, smoking endlessly, while we took our turns to watch over her.

I held Auntie Milly when my mother could not and let her cry, helplessly and hopelessly. And I saw my mother holding Dean in her arms, embracing his strapping young man's body, heard her telling him James could handle it and that he would too, in time. And we do, Anna. We do handle it. There's nothing for it, but to carry on seeing the days through for ourselves the best we can.

Finally we were glad to see her die, glad to let her go into death's oblivion, so that we could cradle her more comfortably in our memories than in our inadequate arms. Life has so many funerals in it, Anna… but joys too… births, marriages, and good loving times. Whether we will or not, we must prepare ourselves to meet both of them - the joy and the distress. They are there both.

Without delay my mother took over the funeral arrangements, ensuring we would once again go through rituals that bring comfort and release, gathering us together at Heritage, making sure we ate and talked and did the ordinary things which assuage heartache. As for me, I sat in the church desperately holding on to the framework of its enduring traditions, listening to the funeral orations, trying to come to terms with the loss of her. James sat in front of me. When he put his arm around Dean, I cried. And I saw you, Anna, outside the church. You put your arms around Dean too. I think it was the first time I realised you were deeply in love with him. How young you were at seventeen, Anna... and how lovely.

Later, when the company had departed, and my mother and Kicker sat with Edward and James and Dean, being with them, listening to them, I went to my waiting place and tried to lose myself in the setting of the sun. Hours later, after the pools of light spilling from each window and each set of doors along the veranda had winked out one by one, James came to me.

"Is that you, Joss?"

"Yes, James." I took his hand and we clung to each other.

"I can't believe she's gone, Titch." I felt the anguish in him and my heart tore in my chest. He was fighting for control.

"Oh, James, what are we going to do without her?"

"I don't know… Hold me, Jossie. Just hold me," he said.

James spent much of the next day, and there always is a next day no matter how long the night, walking in our garden on his own. I watched him from the veranda, seeking the security of my waiting place. The sound of teacups chinking on their saucers interrupted my observations.

"You getting through this okay, Jossie?"

My mother poured the liquid from the pot and picked up a milk jug, settling into the chair beside me.

"I'm more concerned about Auntie Milly and Dean, Mum. Are they managing?'

"Yes. They are. People always do." I looked

up at her carefully. "Don't worry, darling, James will also manage." She knew exactly where I was. Of course. She and I shared the same acute central awareness of these McKelvey men. She poured a second cup. "It's you that's concerning me, Joss," she said gently. I took her hand and, bringing my head down, placed it against my cheek. Her fingers were perfumed with honeysuckle. My tears fell through my mother's hands.

Later, we gathered for tea in the lounge - James and Edward, Kicker and my mother, Hanna, Auntie Milly and Uncle Beau. All the Whitneys and the McKelveys in one room, united in the ceremonies of mourning, with Riaan, the gentle intruder, watching over you, his beloved daughter. You close by Dean's side, trying to absorb the pain of his bereavement; Krivahnen, laying out scones and fruitcake, urging this one to eat a little, another one to take some of his special tea.

James sat alone and apart from the general din of conversation in the main body of the lounge. Lying wearily back in his chair, he looked about him beginning at last to take an interest in mundane things. He was beginning to retreat from his loss. By chance, his eyes fell on a small crystal frog, perfect in every detail. It had lain there for twenty-five years. I moved across the room and sat down beside him.

"You'd better have it back, James. It's been there to take me through all the years... remember?" James smiled slightly, so I picked it up and placed it in his hand. The sun shone through it, so that it gave off points of sparkling light. We looked down on its small perfection.

"Oh, I remember, Joss!" A shadow of intensely reigned-in sadness crossed his face and he stood up. James was leaving me.

"It will need more than a crystal frog, Johanna, to get me through the years she'll not be here," he said bleakly, putting it back in my hand, and returning to the main body of the lounge, he joined with Dean and Edward in conversation.

The immense loss in his voice sent familiar

shadows flickering through my grief. I replaced the crystal frog on the table where it had guarded the passing of time for so long, and looked up. Riaan was watching me from across the room, his eyes narrowed, his face distressed with new awareness – he had just gathered an unforeseen, unexpected knowledge of me and he was going to have to bear it from then on.

CHAPTER NINETEEN

The next weeks were long and lonely. I spent more time than usual on the veranda, trying to work things through. I was worrying about you and Dean. I can't deny that. In the year and a half we had been so utterly caught up with Kerry, I had hardly spent time with you. The two of you had been thrown on one another by what had been happening to Kerry far too often. I had begun to examine my fearful reactions to the fact that I had seen James and myself in you and Dean at Kerry's funeral. I kept seeing how Dean had held you. I knew I had to come to terms with my fears, my loss, my discovery that you were not just my daughter, but a woman in love. And Riaan. Always, there was the problem of Riaan.

How could I tell you to the terrible webs of deception I had fallen into, just like my mother, robbing you of your father in the ensuing silence of the years. My frailties now reared up at me, bringing in every ghost of a past I had almost succeeded in laying. This was the complicated web I had spun out of my own decisions and choices, my own deceptions and silences. How, knowing what I knew, had I not taken better care of you? How did I let it get like this? This was suffering I knew intimately. How could I let it claim you?

No good could come of you loving Dean. James and I were clear proof of that, and Edward and Kicker and Mum. It was not just you that would get hurt. It was all of us. And there was no one but me to tell you so. Perhaps Ella Carney was right. She was always saying I had been too lenient with you, always telling me how much better Peter would have handled you, how much better he would have made you behave.

In becoming like my mother, powerlessness had befallen me. I began to see, in my long hours of restless thinking captured on the veranda of my home, I could not keep from handing on the repetitions in the pattern of our lives by silence and mute hope. Distraught with anxiety, caught up in an inability to broach the issue with you, distressed by an imperative need to reconcile you with Riaan, and the need to decide about Riaan's place in my own life, I paced the length of the moonlit veranda a hundred times, struggling all the while with the grief of Kerry's passing. Riaan's one stricken terrible look, James's one passing comment, had brought such confusion.

How blind people can be Anna, how blind and how stupid! And it seems the closer we are to each other, the less we see.

I knew I should expect Riaan to arrive soon. I wanted to begin the process of unravelling what I had allowed in our lives, but he didn't come. Not immediately. When he did, it was only for dinner at my mother's request. Ella Carney had called, reminding my mother in her inimitable fashion that she had seen her granddaughter only twice in the past year. My mother felt it best that Anna remained at Heritage during the mourning for Kerry, and suggested that the Carneys drive down and spend the night in stead. Ella eagerly seized upon the opportunity.

My mother set about inviting old Uncle

Beau and Auntie Milly, in order to perk them up, or so she said. But I think it was as much a matter of watering down Ella Carney's disruptive effects on company in general, as in sympathy with your straightforward comment that you would rather be with Dean, then spend a weekend with Grandmother Carney. Grandmother Carney can be a bit of a tartar, can't she? I see you agree with me, Anna.

Do you remember, Anna, I called you in to my room, just before they arrived?

"Anna, darling," I said, hesitating.

"What, Mom?" You tossed your head. I was caught by the flawlessness of your skin, the slender defenceless column of your neck.

"Anna, I think you should not be seeing Dean anymore. Anna, I..." You opened your mouth in surprise.

"Don't be silly, mother. I love him." You're like Kicker. You always get straight to the point. You never were one for beating around the bush.

"Anna," I said helplessly. "Please..." You looked at me with that same look you're giving me now. You said, "I don't care, Mother. I don't care what you may have done or not have done, or what my grandmother may have done with Edward Whitney. I don't care about you and James." I drew in a breath. "I'm not blind. I know how you feel about Dean's father. But that doesn't give you the right to take Dean away from me!" You paused and looked directly at me. "I'm not you, Mom," you said bravely, and burst into tears. I took you in my arms.

"Oh, no, you're not, Anna. Oh Anna, I'm sorry darling. I'm so very sorry." I held you until you had done crying, and let you go from me. You did not see my own tears. They came later. My mother and I were finally one. The passing years would lay the same outline on you. This was an inevitability I would not allow. I so badly did not want you to suffer. I would seek a better opportunity for further discussion with you. You were so vulnerable! I sought desperately for the words you needed, Anna, but they did not come. I did not know then my opposition to Dean had more to do with the fact that it would bring James too close to me, than with my fear that you would become yet another unfulfilled Whitney woman.

We had always dressed for formal dinners and that night was no exception. Krivahnen had laid a magnificent table, happy as a sand lark that his considerable culinary mettle was being tested once again. There had been so few dinner parties of late. Kicker stood at the bar, plying old man Carney with whisky and uproarious jokes. Uncle Beau had succumbed well before dinner and lay snoring with gusto on the sofa in the bar area. Auntie Milly and Ella Carney sat perched ever so graciously and ever so properly in the more formal part of the lounge, exchanging salvoes of pleasantries, sipping violently coloured and exotically decorated cocktails. My mother sat back in her chair in her gracious, elegant way, having completed the dinner arrangements, while the two older women circled each others' conversation like birds of prey at the pickings.

Auntie Milly felt a particular claim

regarding Anna, a fact heavily resented by Ella who felt, as paternal grandmother, that Anna had not shown her the respect and obedient love that could be expected and was stabbing spears of mild venom in this regard. She knew you much preferred Aunt Milly to her. I felt mildly sorry for Ella. She obviously had no way of knowing how deceptively formidable an opponent Auntie Milly could be.

"Oh, my dear," heehawed Ella in her way, "I wouldn't dream of wearing anything from Whileworths. So déclassé don't you think?" I arched my inner eyebrow. Déclassé? Ella rattled on. "I only buy from the best Umhlanga boutiques. Definitely nothing at all nice up our way. I see you have the same problem with your clothes."

Uncle Beau gave a hefty snort, recovered briefly and fell back into his comfortable sleep. Auntie Milly shook her net and blinked at Ella, furtively glancing along her own cardigan sleeve to check if a label was showing. She sometimes wore her cardigan inside out. Her face cleared, and I could see she was getting ready to do battle.

"Well, I see you haven't been down to Umhlanga for some time, then, Ella. Couldn't you find something appropriate?" said Auntie Milly pausing to look at Ella's very stylish dress, and then she said sweetly, "Let's face it, Ella, neither none of us is going to make the Thursday page of the papers for fashion sense, are we, dear?"

"Eh... eh, no, ah't nowt thinkit..." Ella inadvertently fell into broad Lancashire accents, but rallied immediately. "Perhaps not you, of cawse, my dear, but Geoffrey Dawkins... we know him well, you know... he *loves* this dress. He's always saying how he can't get over the colours I choose. He's been insisting I have my hair specially done in his very own salon for the Sugar Ball. Hanna, of cawse, always invites us and we always sit at the Whitney table. Don't we, Hanna? We're sure to get a picture in the paper this time. Being the Whitney grandmother has its advantages, you know."

"Whitney grandmother?" Auntie Millie

queried even more innocently, the picture of agreeableness.

"Well... Carney... but you know what I mean, my dear. Ooh, I quite forgot *you* have *recently* married a Whitney," Ella whinnied pointedly. "Bit of a December marriage, without the May part, wouldn't you say... tee hee. *Beau's* a Whitney, isn't he?" Ella patted genteelly at her nose with a white tissue, quite satisfied to have put Milly back in her place. "Anna is *my* granddaughter," she continued in contented tones. "*We're* related. Doesn't that make you more a bit of a distant relative, my dear?" I felt uncomfortable enough to move away.

My thoughts kept returning to you, Anna. Your perceptions of me... how they were going to change that very evening.

"Oh, very distantly related, Ella, but twice over, dearie, twice over... Never mind, though. I'd rather be a friend to Hanna, than a mere relative to her, honey." Auntie Milly scored her triumphant point so neatly that Ella retreated hastily, and they settled down to more reasoned and safer conversations about the issues that really concerned them - recipes, local gossip, and you, Anna, you and your doings. They doted on you equally.

Riaan arrived, bringing his ease around people with him.

"Hello, liefling," he said, after Krivahnen had announced him at the door. He took my hand and looked at me with more than usual directness.

"Riaan, we will have to talk later," I said. He nodded and turned to greet my mother, who was always glad to see him.

"As beautiful as ever, Mrs Whitney." My mother sparkled. Your father does that for people. He has a lovely way with him, Anna.

"Call me Hanna, Riaan. I've told you before," my mother smiled and the patterns of her age fell away from her face to reveal her high-boned, pretty face.

"Johanna, then." He lifted her hand to his lips. "'n Plesier."

"Oh go on with you, Riaan," my mother said, laughing. What a charming person you are,

Riaan Berkhout, I thought, but I could see there was an edge in him. He was holding something in him and it was hurting him very badly. I knew just what it was.

His face lit up as soon as you joined us, Anna. You were still upset. The traces of our earlier conversation marked your face. I could see that, but I was proud of you, the determined way you were controlling your feelings. You were quiet and preoccupied throughout dinner with a new perplexity about the things that brought men and women together. My heart cried out for you, Anna, for my deception of you. There were so many difficult things ahead in your life. I wished I had steered you better through the sands I had fallen into.

"Anna, my dear, young people are so withdrawn these days," said Ella Carney, spearing an asparagus with a fork, looking at me with meaning. I had sat silently throughout the first serving. "Really Anna my dear, can you use more than a few monosyllables. Cheer up a bit for your grandmother, dear! We've all had enough gloom for a while, have we not?" Ella looked significantly at me again. The assembled company began to fall into monosyllables themselves. Ella was beginning to work the conviviality around her, worrying at it like a dog with a rag, destroying it into tatters.

A little later, Ella leaned confidentially towards me. "Do you think Anna should be allowed to wear such a low cut blouse?" she whispered loudly enough for all of us to hear. You looked down at your plate uncomfortably. I answered as steadily as I could,

"I think Anna is old enough to decide for herself, don't you Ella?" You threw down your fork. Wykeford had not as successful with you as the rest of the Whitney girls that passed through their care.

"Leave tha lass be, Ella, she'll be doing no harm," Tim Carney put in mildly.

"May I be excused, mother? Come Dean, let's go for a walk," you said angrily, pulling Dean by the arm. Dean rose to his feet, wiping his mouth with a serviette, a look of concern in his eyes and you left the room.

"What rudeness! Don't you think she's too young to be going off with a young man like that?" Ella niggled on. "In my day, oh we didn't just go off like that. You're far too lenient, Joss. She has no controls. She seems to do just as she pleases. She spends far too much time alone with that boy. You should send her up to the farm more often for some regular discipline."

This was enough for Aunt Milly.

"Listen, Grandmother Carney," she said, "Don't concern yourself about our Anna. She's perfectly fine." Auntie Millie fuelled herself with a nip of brandy for her coup dé gras and drew a breath to deliver her next words with as much cutting edge as she could muster. "Anna does what she pleases just to get out of your hearing range, my dear." Ella gasped. "Dean's a fine boy. She loves him. He loves her. That needn't concern you, Ella... or anyone else," Millie continued fiercely, glaring around the table. "You just leave them be." Ella opened and closed her mouth a couple of times, looking around the table. We sat stiffly, looking at her. Kicker was smiling broadly.

"My dear," she gasped, "My dear..." Mercifully, Krivahnen announced coffee in the lounge, and shortly afterwards the older people retired for the night, leaving Riaan and me in the lounge.

"Well, liefling, what is it? Anna is very upset tonight." The warm golden light spilled from the chandelier and threw up reflections on the ivory ceiling, flicking in and out of revolving blades of the fans.

"Riaan, I..." He picked up a cigarette, flicked his lighter and waited silently. He seemed hard and aloof. "Riaan, what about Anna? How am I going to tell her about you?" He waited a little and said,

"What else do you have to tell her? And why now, after all this time... anyway, isn't there something you should first be telling me?" I fell silent. What could I say that would not pull us all apart anyhow? "Well then, Joss, let me tell you," Riaan continued, "Why don't you marry me?" He took my arm and cupped my chin forcing me to look at him. "What can I do to persuade you? Do you love him, Joss? Do you love him that much?"

"Riaan," I said, "Riaan. I was so lonely when I met you. You brought me such companionship... then, and now. You've brought me so much meaning..."

"But..." he said, with difficulty.

"Riaan, you brought me Anna. You gave me Anna. She is my life's gift, Riaan. She's the only thing that makes any sense." I was utterly desperate to give him no further hurt.

"And mine too, Joss. She's my gift too, but... you cannot give me you, né, dearest. You will not have me. You will not give yourself to me. You did not then, and you will not now." I nodded mutely.

"Does the fact that I am Anna's father not change things a little, *liefling?* Ah, I see not..." We both turned to the door. You had cried out, Anna. We did not know you had been standing there.

"What's he saying, Mamma? What does he mean?" The gathering place of my being tore itself apart. This night had been too tormented. I was afraid you would not recover from it. I held out my hand.

"Anna, I have done you a great wrong," I said. "I should have told you years ago."

"But my dad? Peter, my dad?" You twisted this way and that, struggling with shock and knowledge. I bit back my own cry of pain.

"Oh Anna. I'm so sorry. I'm so sorry."

"Steady now, Anna, *skat*," Riaan interjected as I reached for you, but, remember, you pushed me away.

"Liar! You're lying to me! You lie about everything, Mom. Everything!" Before I could hold you and clasp you in my arms and explain to you, you ran from the door. Riaan held me back.

"Leave her, Johanna. She needs to come to terms with this in her own way. She will work things through in her own time. You know what, Joss? You are going to learn to love me. For Anna's sake." I shook my head.

"I can't, Riaan. I can't," I whispered. "It's too late for that. I'm too damaged. Please, Riaan, don't let me hurt you like this. I can only hurt you worse, hurt her even more! I care about you so much. You are my friend. Riaan, oh Riaan, my heart fell to pieces too long ago for you to be able to pick them up. I can't stand between you and Anna. But you have to see that Peter stands between us... you, Riaan, and me. He's always there in the shadows, between you and me." There was a pause as we struggled for composure.

"Not Peter, Anna," said Riaan gently. "James. James stands between you and me." He rose, hopeless defeat on his face. I put my head down on the arm of the sofa and cried as if there would be no end of weeping. I heard the door close gently.

At length, I stood up and switched off the light, immersing the brilliant room in inky darkness. I stepped through the doors and looked up at the impossible moon pinned to the vast indigo sky above the veranda. How does anyone know what to do? I asked. Who's going to show me what to do now? The branches of the great wild fig clattered together. I knew I should have to go to you, Anna, and comfort you as my mother had once done me, in spite of her own distress, her own tearing, aching heart. I walked slowly along the veranda and hesitated before the entrance to your bedroom.

The door stood open, abandoned to the night. On the bed you lay, Anna, naked, oblivious to everything but the insistence of Dean's arching young body and your own crucial need to love him utterly.

CHAPTER TWENTY

Oh Anna, there is no need to look at me like that! I'm a woman. You and I have felt the same things, done the same things. I never did tell you what I had seen. It was not necessary. In that one act, you crossed the threshold when first a girl becomes her mother, and from that point on, a mother relates to her daughter only as a woman, for the rest of their lives. I felt, in those first seconds of shock and denial, an unexpected acceptance of these issues. Without a word, I walked away from this act of yours, this recurring Whitney act, this inability of ours to love within the bounds of sanctity, an act neither deliberate nor inadvertent. We were just so, you, my mother, me. We were formed by each other, not for this, but out of this… and from love, we were made for just this enactment. But this was love's form. It was love's form. And that had nothing to do with reality. You were much too young for this. You were taking busy chances that may have trapped you in a waiting place too long for you to sustain. Dean would have to go.

As I hurried back to the lounge, I reflected that you had chosen a path different from mine. Dean was not James. You were not me. You would not lie down without a fight. By doing what you had done, I knew you were telling me you deserved your own way of being. I recognised your courage, felt your strength. However, Anna, I also believed you had to make decisions drawn on your experience, as well as your love, and it was up to me to help you do that.

If anyone had erred, it had been me. I had not been open with my mother, or with you. In fact, I had not been open with anyone. Right from the start, lacking your brave confrontation and insistence on resolution, I had brought you to this point just as surely as if I had planned it. I would have to start making decisions of honesty and choices of integrity so that I could protect you from the consequences of being my daughter... in a way my mother had never protected me. I would have to involve James. He would have to help me help you confront the questions ahead of us. He would have to help us stop the recurring Whitney-McKelvey McKelvey-Whitney pattern in our lives. And this pattern, I resolved, as I entered the darkened lounge, was going to end.

An outraged hiss from the darkness within the room made me start.

"Oh no, you will not! You will not!" the voice insisted, piercing the gloom. I reached for the switch and flooded the room with light. Ella Carney burst into the room propelled by an umbrella in her back, behind which Aunt Milly's incensed face bobbed. "You stay out of Anna's life, Ella Carney, or I will personally whack you out of this house with this!" Auntie Milly gave Ella another vicious poke with the umbrella and they came to a skidding halt, blinking in the sudden abundance of light, their ample bosoms heaving.

"Well I never! Well I never did!" gasped Ella Carney, throwing her hands up as she stumbled forward.

"Milly! Ella!" I exclaimed. "What *are* you doing?" Milly was beside herself with rage. She stood panting for words, which were not forthcoming, her outrage undiminished by my sudden appearance. Ella squeaked as Milly gave the umbrella another jab, and skipped out of the way with alacrity, realising that I offered some protection from further outrage.

"Do you know what those two young people are up to?" Ella managed in scandalised tones, despite her involvement with the umbrella's whereabouts.

"No, we don't! But you do, you spying, interfering old bat," cried Auntie Milly.

"An' you'll do now't abaht it, will you? My own granddaughter! In bed like a hoor!" Milly lifted the umbrella in spite of my restraining hand. She was speechless with rage. Ella turned to me bitterly. "I've always known it. My Peter was too good for the likes of the Whitneys. Under this roof! Right beneath all our noses! Your daughter carrying on just like you did with Peter. Right here under our noses."

"Noses! Noses! The only nose that needs mentioning now is the one that has been poking in business which is none of your concern, Ella Carney!"

"Calm down, Auntie Milly," I managed to say. Aunt Milly would not be stopped.

"Making me think there's burglars about. You silly woman! I nearly had a heart attack! Do you think I wanted to wake my poor dear Beau? He needs all the rest he can get, you know, hey? Do you think I wanted to frighten him? And what do I find creeping down the passage but this ridiculous prying old snoop. And me a defenceless old woman with only a useless weapon for protection!" Auntie Milly brandished the umbrella. Mercifully, Ella Carney skipped out of its range and stood peering at full alert for any further possible incursions from its sharp point. "What do I find?" Auntie Milly was not to be diverted. "What do I find, but Ella Carney in the passageway? Trying to listen at Anna's door, weren't you? Now this... Calling Anna a prostitute are you? Take this, you old coot! "

Milly danced with indignation, her face red with anger and exertion, intent on whacking Ella with another shot.

"I was only going for a drink of water. Then I heard something. I was only trying to make sure," Ella protested feebly, looking helplessly in my direction for support. She backed away carefully.

"Now, listen, both of you," I said. "Sit down. Auntie Milly, recover yourself. Ella, Milly's quite right. What Anna is up to is none of your business. You have no right to call Anna anything. Come, Milly, sit down, please. You will have to let Anna be, Ella. I will take care of Anna. This matter concerns only the two of us, and the McKelveys. Please let this business drop, Ella. Now, let's get a cup of coffee from the kitchen and be sensible. Come, Milly, would you prefer a small toddy?" Ella sniffed, but I was rewarded with a smile from Auntie Milly.

"Sorry, Ella, lovie. I really thought you were a burglar," she said in an attempt to mollify Ella, now that she had calmed down. Ella sniffed again.

"Well, you shouldn't bash people about with that umbrella of yours, Millicent," Ella answered, rapidly beginning with the process of salvaging her pride.

"Don't creep about then listening at doors then," was Milly's tart reply, and they set about the business of getting some drinks from the kitchen, the umbrella lying forgotten on the lounge carpet.

I stayed sat back in an armchair, wrung out by the events of the night. All I could think about was the heartbreaking picture of you, Anna, of how you and Dean seemed to fit each other, and what lay ahead of us, as a result. We finished our drinks and went to our rooms, each to lie awake struggling with our different concerns in our different ways.

I called James and asked him to visit me after dinner the following evening, knowing my parents were taking Dean and Anna to the theatre and that we would be alone. I was nervous. I could not refrain from twisting my handkerchief through my hands or from pacing up and down until he arrived. I had rehearsed what I needed to say a hundred times but I knew it was going to be difficult.

Krivahnen announced James. James gave him a hearty slap on the shoulder.

"Krivahnen, you old so and so. What have you been up to lately?" It was a greeting of familiarity and long acquaintance. Krivahnen shook James's hand warmly. He set out the teacups and gave the spotless drinking glasses a final polish.

"I'll be finishing now, Miss Joss."

"Thanks for staying back, Krivahnen. I'll see you tomorrow." He looked at me approvingly, almost giving me a wink, and then departed for his journey home. James poured himself a beer and settled comfortably in an armchair. He seemed to belong there.

"What do you want to talk to me about, Titch?" he asked.

"James," I said as evenly as I could, "I want you to tell Dean to stop seeing, Anna." Startled, James took in a breath, and looked bewildered.

"Are the seeing each other? I mean I know they've always been friends... like you and I were, Titch..."

"They're more than friends, James," I said gently. "It's inevitable, I suppose. They spend so much time together. They're young. These things happen." James gave an oath and stood up to pace on the floor between us.

"I'm going to clout that lad to Cape Town and back again! He knows better than to lay a hand on Anna. I taught him better than that!"

"That's not the issue, James. The issue is that they are serious about each other... you and I both know no good can come of that..."

"What do you mean, Joss?" I looked up at James uncomprehendingly. Surely he knew. Surely he knew about my mother and his father. He was frowning, puzzled.

"Your father..." I began, searching for the right words, desperate not to cleave him with all the things we had had to bear as a result of my mother's liaison with his father. A shadow crossed his face. And he tossed his head angrily, saying, "My father? Oh... I see... You mean you think Dean isn't good enough for the likes of the Whitneys? Now, where have I heard that before?"

I could not believe his words. Was it possible that James was not aware of the strong dislike between our families? Had Edward or Sarah never discussed these matters? What *had* passed between him and Kicker all those years ago? I was aghast.

"You know, Joss," James continued. His voice was low and uncertain, his face hurt with memory.

"My father once sent me away because he said you were too young for a nineteen year old boy to be seeing. You were such a sweet kid. We had such fine times together. Oh God... I was just your friend, Joss. I wasn't *seeing* you." I looked down at the floor. James had never been just a friend to me. What shame had they thrust on him on my account?

"Then your father got hold of me when I got back from the States, that was years later, and told me to stay away from you. He accused me of robbing the cradle and said he had once thrashed my father for laying a hand on your mother. He found them together, you know... your mum and my dad... that's why they sent me away... I've had to live with that! I've had to deal with their affair all these years! I had to see my mother dealing with it. He was going to thrash me with a riding crop if he ever found me near you. And then he did! Remember that night at the stable? Your dad was fond of using that thing when he couldn't get his own way! And you know, Titch, you know what's worse? I've had to deal with how that made you feel about me." I could not bear the pain in his voice.

"James..."

"No, Titch. I've always held back in deference to these feelings of yours. I've always put you first. I've respected you, and your family, in every way possible. But to know that you let our parents' rubbish affect you to the extent where you colour Dean with the same brush? Well, that's hard. You never could find time for me after your Dad got hold of me and cut me with that crop of his. He made sure we did not see each other again. Kicker did that twice to me, Joss, twice! You never looked at me again! But to do the same to Dean? And to Anna! I thought I knew you better than that, Johanna!" I could not find my voice.

"That's not the way it was, James..." I began.

"Wasn't it? How was it then, Joss? Tell me!"

How do you tell the man you love, utterly, with the extent of your being, that you have desired him more than life itself? How do you do that without the wrongdoing of his wife, his mother, his father... my father, my mother? I was angry with him. How could he believe I did not want to see him? I took the same resolution I had once taken at Peter's graveside. I would take care of this on my own. This had to stay with me. It had to finish with me. I would only hurt James by admitting that I loved him beyond feeling, beyond reason. "James," I said.

"Just take Dean away. Just get him away. This is no good for any of us. It never has been."

James's face darkened. Oh, I had seen him like that... only once when Kicker had found us after their argument, and I had been trying to get him to kiss me and Kicker had thrashed him with a crop. James stood silent, his face flushing, and, then, seeming to pull himself from the edge of his own destruction, he said angrily, "Very well, Johanna. If that's what you want...that is best, then." He turned on his heel and walked out into the gathering darkness that was folding the night like a cotton sari over the roof above us. Sometimes, like the wild spiders, we cry together without any tears.

Dean was sent to learn the sugar trade in the southern plantations of America soon after that. Do you remember, Anna, how you came to my room each year at the Christmases after that night, and said, "Mother, I'm going to wait for Dean. You can't take him away from me. He's going to wait for me. It won't take forever." You said it deliberately, not defiantly, so that I would take it in and remember it. And once a year in August, you would come in and say, "Dean's back, mother. I'm having dinner with him. I will be back late." What's a mother to say to an adult daughter that will keep her from the pain she is gathering up for herself? There was nothing either James or I could do about you and Dean, Anna. Life is full of anger and pain. No matter that I told you how it had been between Hanna, my mother, and Edward your grandfather... and Dean's. You were strong and your road was yours to forge you said. Well, we have to get on and just deal with these things our own way, don't we?

Don't you smile at me like that! Mothers also make mistakes, Anna.

It's getting late. I will have to get on with the story. You should be getting a good night's sleep. I'm pleased you are happy, my darling... now, that's the last of the lace panels adjusted. This dress is just about done. Oh Anna, what a beautiful bride you will be. Any way let me get on with the story.

CHAPTER TWENTY ONE

Kicker had begun to limp severely, and to snatch for air, laboriously and painfully, to feed his failing heart. It made the time with him increasingly precious and necessary. I saw it in my mother's eyes, the concern for him, the sure knowing that only the hard stubborn ridges of him were holding him up as his body wore away beneath him.

One evening, as we sat on the veranda in the usual splendid drama of the setting sun, he reached across to me and, placing his hand on my forearm, said, "Joss, you'll look after your mother, won't you?"

"Oh Dad, of course," I replied as steadily as I could, fighting the contraction of my throat.

"It was not your mother's fault, you know," he continued. I sat silent, wanting to know, dreading confirmation of what he was about to tell me. James's hard dark face lay like a replica of pain in the walls of my being. I had not seen him at all, except in restless disturbed regretful dreaming, for the past two years.

"What, Dad?" I asked. "What was not her fault?"

But he had retreated into the confusion of age, the long hard years of his memories and experiences and dreams lying heavy on him.

"Eh," he said, "It's time. It's time to go in. Where's Hanna? Hanna, where are you, my darling heart?" My mother emerged from the blurred syrupy light of the lounge and put her arms around him, helping him to his feet. They walked along the length of the veranda through the long slatted doors that led into their bedroom.

When they did that, it threw me back to the times I used to stand in front of the very same doors in the dawn, until my mother called, "Come, Jossie. Come in, precious," and I would climb up beside her and lie in her arms and feel the warm hollows Kicker had left, and wonder if he was already riding away astride his horse, the centre of my universe, and master of all he surveyed.

On one of those concerned evenings, I discovered what had really happened between my parents and the McKelveys those long years ago. I was given an explanation that finally made sense of things. Oh, Anna, it's so hard to talk about it... you know how a single decision, acted upon, creates the need for another, and another... until a life...whole lives, are woven out of choices. That a single event can have so many intertwined consequences!

Rays of last light fanned out along the edges of veranda bougainvillaea to form a shadowed framework against the swirling lavenders and deep maroons spilling out along the horizon. A mango-scented breeze drifted in from the sea, picking up bouquets of masala and avocado as it swept through the estate. The fig tree clattered, shaking breeze from its leaves and scattering figs about. Dry fig leaves lay like crackling on the lawns, rolling this way and that

I had been distracted and uneasy all day.

My mother had been out on the veranda at sunrise as I was leaving. She wanted me to call in at Dr Moffat's clinic on my rounds through the plantation.

"Kicker didn't get up at all yesterday, Joss. It's not like him. I'm really anxious, darling," she had said gravely. When I returned at the end of the day, my mother did not join me for a drink, as was her habit.

"The doctor has been in attendance of Master Kicker, Miss Joss, all of the day. It is a matter for worrying, indeed," Krivahnen said when he had placed the silver tray on the table beside me while I waited on the veranda, his face disturbed and troubled. "The serving of supper is in an half hour, Miss Joss."

"Thanks, Krivahnen. I can see you're concerned. He's had a bad day, hasn't he?" Krivahnen sighed.

"Krivahnen, do you think he is going. Do you think my father is going?"

"That day of going is set, Miss Joss. Just as is the day of arriving. But it is as the falling of the figs. We come. We go. Don't cry, Miss, don't cry. It is as it has to be." He put out his delicately muscled pale brown hand and I clung to it.

A while later, I walked along the veranda, past the eight sets of French doors and their stained glass panels, each pair an entrance to a bedroom flanking the western edge of the house. This was my home, this Edwardian sweep of rooms laid in three rows, the bedrooms, the inner lounges and entertainment rooms, and the functional kitchens and studies and workrooms that looked out on to the back lawns and gardens. These peaked corrugated roofs, jutting from outer walls over the filigreed verandas to lean out on white bougainvillaea-clad columns of cement... these had enclosed Kicker all his life... just as they had me.

The debris of your university texts and CD's lay scattered on the chequered veranda table, Anna, as my own books and records had done more than two decades ago. It was inconceivable to think of Heritage without Kicker. I knocked your bedroom, this room with the pressed metal ceilings and intricate fans, and the mosquito netting frames, the one I had left as a bride, and returned to as a mother, preparing for the birth of her child. There you lay in the carved oaken bed of my own young days, Anna, sleepy and beautiful. I stroked your cheek, closed and bolted the tall doors behind me, and walked down the veranda again.

Night had fallen fully, dense and black. Shadows leant heavily into the house. Only the sugary light that fell in blurred pools onto the veranda floor outside my parents' room relieved their silhouetted intimidating presences. Death was closing in on us.

Passing the deep open window of my parents' room, I was arrested by the sound of my mother speaking urgently and quickly. I came to a halt, caught again in one of those vaulting moments that sometimes still suspended me in a black web of confusion and loss.

"Kicker. Kicker, darling... you have to try. Sit up, darling. Sit up. Don't leave me like this. Don't leave me." I heard him stir at my mother's urgent words, and my mother's chair creaking as she leant to take his hand. His low voice, cracked with suffering, drew me inexorably to the window and I looked in, filled with loss and apprehension. He had his hand on my mother's head, where she had laid it against his chest. Her hair was so white, her face so fine and fragile.

"Hanna, darling. There's something you must do," he said painfully. My mother stifled her crying.

"Hanna, tell Jossie about Edward, will you? Tell her what happened… She thinks Edward is her father, you know. It's buggering up things… like it always did." My mother sat up and all the masks she had ever worn fell from her face. She was stricken.

"Oh, dear God, no! No, Kicker. Edward isn't her father. You know that, Kicker!"

My father continued from his place of agony, "Ah, do I? Do I, Hanna? I never was sure…" He was struggling to speak, gasping in short laboured breaths. "Finding the two of you like that. Oh God, Hanna, you broke my heart. You broke my heart." The cry that rose from my mother held all the pain of the years of her guilt.

"I never went back again. I stood by you. I stood by *you*, Kicker. I'm so sorry... oh Kicker, oh, Kicker, what a terrible life it is. I know whose daughter she is. *She* knows."

"Ah, is it so? Is it not as she believes?" My father spoke with immense difficulty. My mother put her face into her hands, tears slipping through her fingers.

"When you came in on us, Kicker... oh Lord, Kicker... when you came in on us... he had not made love to me. I've told you that. I've told you so many times. Why do you not believe me?" Her voice was agitated, full of loss. I remained frozen in this new discovery about my mother, caught at the window, realising what I had been afraid of all these years.

"But you loved him, Hanna. You loved him," my father said.

After a silence, she answered. I could see the tears of her face. She was broken, open. I knew she would be truthful. In all the years after that time my father had walked in on my mother and her lover to find him deep in her nakedness, she had been true. True to him, true to her word... and to me. She had never again felt the touch of her lover's hand. I stood at the window my tears falling unheeded. I wish I had known. I wish I had known how brave my mother had been. I would not have been so hard on her. My mother lifted my father's hand to her cheek and said gently, "Yes, I did love him, Kicker. I still do. Not a day that has gone by that I have not thought of him, darling."

Kicker sank back into his pillows, his eyes on her, desperate and appealing. My mother continued, her voice gentle and resolute. "You see, Kicker, dearest heart, I found that there are many kinds of loving, and that the best kind comes out of endurance. The best rises out of being faithful... out of promises steadily held... that kind of love came through you, Kiernan, not Edward." She paused, searching for the right words and then smiled. "We learned to depend on each other, didn't we, Kiernan? On each other's honour. Look how we weathered the storms, dearest. The years brought us together in the heart. That's where it matters. My heart betrayed you, Kiernan, but never my deeds... I learned to depend on that, on the promise I made you that night. And then you became my reward, darling... if we could go back again and change things I would not, Kicker, I would not. Doing so would mean that I would never have known the richness of you. You would never have loved me the way you have. Oh, Joss is your daughter all right. Same chip, same granite." My mother gave a shaky laugh and raised her eyes to look at my father.

A look of deep regret crossed his face.

"All these years... I didn't know..." he said. "I really hurt you that night, Hanna... I never trusted you the same way again... I hurt you so badly. I hurt you then, and I wanted to go on hurting you. I should not have done that. I should not have hit you... used my riding crop on you in that terrible way. I should have thrashed him only. I've wanted to say I am sorry for that, all these years. I've wanted to know that you truly forgave the rage and pain that made me beat you and him like that... Oh Hanna, Hanna, dearest..." My mother sat up and pulled her blouse from her shoulders. Gently she lay beside him, picked his hand up and put it to her scarred breast.

"Hush, Kiernan. Don't upset yourself. Rest now, darling. Rest now. It's all right. It's all right. It doesn't matter, Kiernan, it doesn't matter." A look of contentment flashed in his eyes, and he relaxed against her body.

I leaned against the wall, the terrible vision of my father thrashing my mother in her nakedness and shame vivid in my own shocked heart. So many things began to make sense. After a little, I heard his voice again.

"We had some times, didn't we, Hanna?"

"Yes, we did, dearest. We did."

"Call Jossie in now. I'm so tired... See me through here, darling. Help me through. Are you there, Hanna? Hanna? Ah, it's you Jossie. Here you are, my own daughter." I wanted to reach past the dark thick walls of death and pull him back, so that he could hold me once again and say, "You, okay with this, girl? It's not too late to change your mind, you know." And I wanted to tell him that I had changed my mind, I had changed my mind. But he was already dead, the last breath rattling in his throat.

Oh, I miss Kicker still! I read a poem, once, Anna. I remember recalling fragments of it, as we stood at Kicker's graveside... about how fathers could not shield their children, how we become like a lot of wild spiders, crying together, without any tears. I don't remember who wrote that poem now, Anna. Won't you turn up the light a little? It's getting late and I think we need some coffee.

CHAPTER TWENTY TWO

Kicker's funeral, the third in our family, was different from Peter's and Kerry's. I don't know why it should be de rigueur to wear black at funerals. This time, it seemed to me, we needed to wear white. We should have been celebrating Kicker's release from the small cage existence had become for him. His failing body had forced him to a place where there was no riding of swift horses, where no one heeded his roared laughter, where the wind had ceased to move across his face, and no sun shone. In heaven's sweeping light I wanted him to find a place called Heritage. Now, it was my turn to support my mother as she stood beside his grave, a flood of unheeded tears covering her upturned face, her hands clasped at her sides. She would no longer wait for Kicker on the veranda, at her waiting place, sipping tea from a fluted white cup, watching the setting of the sun in a copper sky. He was no longer there. He would never again place himself between me and my nightmares, holding me on his huge shoulder, asking, "You okay with that?" in that wonderful gruff way of his.

Next to my mother stood Edward McKelvey, head bowed and reflective, relief and respect fighting for dominance of his craggy features. To the left of him, James. How deeply the years were beginning to lie in his serious weather-beaten, time-beaten face. I remember quite clearly how he placed his hand on Dean's shoulder and that Dean held you at the waist, Anna, the experienced suffering of his own mother's passing making him turn to you to murmur heartfelt words.

Thus we said goodbye to Kicker, each in our own way. I became conscious of overwhelming gratitude. This was my father. He had not passed on without leaving himself behind in me. The way I looked and acted, my Irish-grey eyes, my stubborn, stubborn will, these were his inadvertent legacy. But the way I loved, could love, did love, this he had taught me. Painstakingly, carefully, from the heart of his hurt, he had loved me, no matter what. With his faults and his strength, he had demanded love, and had claimed it. Had given it. "Sure, I'm okay with this, Dad," I said quietly. My mother reached for my hand and I clung to it. He had loved us both. Perhaps his faults had been his strength. Mine were.

It was time, then, to assuage our mourning, being with each other, joined for a while in the partaking of the rituals, of sharing memories in the lounge, which had seen us gathered together in the losses of Peter and Kerry, and now of my own father. I looked up to see Riaan watching me, his arms folded across his chest, sad and serious. I smiled at him. No wonder Kicker had liked him so much. But, it was James who held my arm and saw me to the car. It was James I clung to in loss and grief. This was the way it has always been.

In the long liquid light of the sinking afternoon, I withdrew to return to my waiting place. From the veranda, I could see the assembled company through the windows of the lounge. Edward was closest to me. He stood beside my mother, determined, uncertain, his eyes never leaving her face. My mother was smiling slightly at his words. I knew they were talking about Kicker. Grief had not yet allowed her to admit that their time had finally come. I could not help the vaulting of my heart. I realised that my own life had brought me to the point where I could allow them that. My mother deserved no less from me. And you and Dean, Anna, stood further down the room, fitting together like the pieces of a jigsaw, locked and keyed, one against the other, making meaningless the years I had forced separation upon you. My mind took in the picture of the two of you, standing so close, so at one with each other.

I could not help a shock of recognition flooding through me. Suddenly I could see James. I could see me. So we must have been. So we must have looked when first we found the love between us. Hanna and Kicker and Edward and Sarah, Auntie Milly and Beau - they had all seen James and me, just as I saw you and Dean, young and resolute, joined together at the hip, perfectly belonging, reflecting the weaving patterns that they themselves had spun for us. Why was it that they pulled us apart? For that matter, why had I held you and Dean apart? I stood up from my chair in distress and walked along the veranda. Where was James? James and I, the broken part of the pattern, the ends that would never meet. I covered my face with my hands.

"Come on, *liefling*, come inside now. Don't grieve. He's all right now." It was Riaan, standing in the shadow cast on the flagstones by the falling light from the bougainvillaea.

"How am I going to get through the years ahead without him, Riaan?" I asked him and he thought I meant Kicker.

"Never mind, *liefling*. Kicker's fine now. Let me hold you. Lean on me a bit." And so James found me, clinging to Riaan, adrift and perfectly alone, weeping for lost things, lost lives, and lost, lost love. He stood hesitantly at the door. Before I could let Riaan go and call his name, he had walked away down the steps and away through the crackling of fig leaves that lay scattered in red and gold profusion across the lawn. A lover was always leaving. Some lover was always leaving.

CHAPTER TWENTY THREE

"What's up, Mum?" I asked. In the half-light, her pale hair drenched in bronze, she was a young woman again, alert and seeking approval. I could imagine her at the height of her beauty and grace. She was nervous and busied herself pouring drinks, settling herself down in the wicker chair beside me. I put my hand out encouragingly. She smiled slightly and said, "I have something to ask you, Joss." I leaned forward to listen. I had been expecting the news. I knew better than anyone how long, and how brief, six months of waiting could be.

"Would you mind very much if you were to be on your own at Heritage with Anna? I..."

"Mother," I said. "Let's make this a little easier for us both. When are you and Edward getting married?" She laughed and I was charmed that her voice sounded so shy. "Are you asking permission?"

Joss... really... you're so straightforward... Well, do you mind, darling?" I took her hand.

"Mum, I'm delighted. Kicker would approve, you know." She relaxed slightly, then sat forward earnestly, a look of appeal crossing her face.

"There's so little time left, Joss. Life's too short for the waiting." I hesitated. It was important for me to undo some of the pain I had caused her by my own decisions and choices.

"Sometimes waiting is the only thing, Mum, it's the only thing there is... until the confusion clears and we know how we *should* be. You've waited so long for me to grow up, to see things as they really are."

Presently she said, "Would next week be too soon?"

"No, Mother, next week is not too soon... especially for Edward, eh?"

"Don't be sly, Jo." My mother laughed. In that laughter was the flowing harmonic of a perfect piece of music.

"And you? What about you? Why don't you marry that charming man of yours, Joss? You could do worse than Riaan. Your happiness is of great concern to me.”

“I know that, Mother, I know… but I decided a long time ago I would not marry Riaan. I cannot.”

“But why, dearest? It’s incomprehensible to me that you continue to choose sitting here on this veranda night after night, year after year, on your own in complete solitude.” She paused, then, with revelation dawning in her, she cried, “You do not have to be like this, Johanna. You do not have to be like me! ” Her cry affected me more deeply than she knew. I held my hand up. She sat waiting in the darkness, listening most intently.

“I have something to tell you. I should have told you long before. Perhaps, I wouldn’t have been brought here to this place… you know, this place of waiting… this wasted waiting life of mine…” She gave a cry.

“You’ve been so alone all these years… it’s been so much harder for you than I expected. Oh, what have I made you carry all this time?”

“No, you made me carry nothing. It’s of my own making. I had an affair with Riaan just before Peter died, Mum." I heard a soft intake of breath in the obscured light.

"Anna's father... Yes, I see... I've had some idea for a while... I've wondered..."

"We should have talked long before all this, Mum, we should have talked."

"I see that. I see that. Oh, Jossie, how could you have borne all this alone for all this time?"

"You did, Mum. You bore your faithlessness by yourself. You did not share that with me! Not once. Not once."

My mother fell into an agitated silence.

"Oh, Joss... oh, Joss..." she said eventually. "Not by myself. I had Kicker. I have Edward. They bore my faithlessness with me. They loved me anyhow."

"I loved you, too, Mum! I love you, too! Even if you didn't want to, you shared everything with me anyhow. I lived it too! I live it now. This faithlessness, this dreadful faithlessness that removes my love from me." She lay her face on my hands and her tears fell on my fingers. The fragrance of honeysuckle that lay in her hair was sweet and encompassing. We clung to each other. Mother and daughter we were.

I was so glad her waiting was over.

In a while, she poured two large drinks from the tray and placed a glass in my hand.

"I'd better start from the beginning, Johanna," she said, and she began to tell me everything I have told you today.

In return, I was finally able to say all the things I had wanted to say to my mother since I was nine years old. She took in each part of my long account through that long night with murmurs of compassion and recognition, listening as one finding a fellow traveler on a long and arduous road… she listened much as you have listened to me all day. And there was release in the sharing, relief and closeness.

When it was done, she said, "So, it's James you care for. You love him still! Here's the pattern we can do nothing about. We can only negotiate it. Dean and Anna. Edward and me. You and James!"

"No," I said sadly. "Not James and me. We're

the parts of the pattern that don't belong. He doesn't feel the same way about me. He's made that quite clear. Having Anna with Riaan has somehow diverted the strands... changed the design..."

There was a long silence.

"You're sure about that, darling? Surely it could change? You could change it. You are heartbroken, Joss. Change it!" I shook my head in the darkness. I did not want to shed any more tears.

"No, Mother, this is where it ends. It ends with James and me." She did not answer. I was grateful for her innate, fluid awareness. An overwhelming pain made it impossible for me to continue talking.

CHAPTER TWENTY FOUR

You remember the quiet ceremony, attended by Beau, Millicent, Riaan, James, Dean, and the two of us, don't you, Anna? As we entered the courts, I caught my mother's hand. She turned to look at me.

"You look lovely, Mum. I'm so pleased for you."

"I know you are, Jossie. Thank you. Thank you so much, darling." Serene and beautiful at seventy, she was as much in love as it is possible for a woman to be.

"Tell her, Joss. Tell Anna everything. Do what I didn't," she said quietly. As he touched her arm, and indicated that they should begin the proceedings, the smile she gave Edward got me round to thinking that God was, indeed, in His heaven.

And Uncle Beau! Honestly! Do you remember how he kept congratulating you and Dean, in stead of Edward and Gran, however often Aunt Milly told him that you two were only getting married later in the year. He insisted on taking James aside every so often and saying confidentially, "Well, old sock, wot about making a McKelvey out of Joss here. May as well, me lad! She's a good wench, a good one! Rides like a divil, y'know. V'ry good in a wife that, old boy, ain't it? Tell me... what's wrong with you, cockie? Why don't you marry her? If I were twenny years younger, and didn't hev m'old girl here..." He managed to take in that James was getting distinctly uncomfortable in the face of these heartfelt comments, but his tone of encouragement remained unmistakable. "I'd give you a run f'r the money, young fellow... never could understand you McKelvey blokes...you chaps never..."

"You just concentrate on your job, Uncle Beau," I interrupted severely, my face flaming.

My mother merely smiled and glanced up at Edward for the hundredth time that day. Edward could not hide his amusement. He placed his arm round my mother and waited, like most of the assembled company, to hear what Beau would say next.

"Job? Job? Wot job? Oh! I see… giving away the bride here. That's the job, ain't it?" He rallied rapidly. "An' wot 'n honour, it is. An honour. Should hev done it years ago, Hanna, years ago… 'fore you and that Irish fellow… now wot's his name…" he proceeded down yet another slippery conversational slope. Milly gave Beau a sharp poke in the ribs with her elbow. He began searching desperately for both the breath and the understanding to do what was required of him.

"You talk too much, Beau," Milly scolded, and straightened his tie lovingly.

Then, after the ceremony, my mother left with Edward in a flurry of confetti, good wishes, and a blaze of sunlit happiness.

It was hard to settle down after that. Although they were no more than a ten minute walk away, and I visited them as often as possible, Heritage was empty. You and Dean flew in and out, as young people do, but the nights were long and filled with memories. Riaan was often there. I liked his company, but, always, when he left I felt let down and alone.

I could not fend off the increasing loneliness that crept in at sunset and only left when the morning's hard riding took care of this disturbing propensity towards self-pity. I seemed to be crying a lot, much like a spider without any tears.

Sometimes I began to think that companionship was enough to go by. Perhaps I should marry Riaan. Perhaps his friendship was enough to tie the two of us together into a more permanent arrangement? I was almost fifty. It was ridiculous that I seemed to be holding out for some absurd romantic impossibility. And always, when these moods came upon me, I would see Peter, see his hurt, closed face. He seemed to be saying," You loved him, Joss. *Him.* Why did you marry me?"

Krivahnen became especially important to my wellbeing at that time. He is full of wisdom, that man.

I loved to hear him speaking of early Heritage days when Kicker strode the fields of cane and beautiful dancers wove their steps through bright Divali evenings to the sounds of sitar and drums. The stories he told of the many-limbed gods were shot through with sense and philosophy. He knew such interesting things. He knew of the women bearing breyani that left a glow in the belly and wedding headdresses glittering in the sun. And, although he did not say it, he knew of the woman who greeted her lover behind the temple. The weddings, the funerals, the friends, the enemies... he remembered them all. And, of course, he never stopped talking about you.

When it got late, he would move from window shutter to door, fastening everything in its place, his hands shaking with age, making sure I was safe and secure for the night and bid me good night. I wait for a while and then retreat from waiting into restless sleep, restless, restless remembering, until morning called me back to the loss of awareness I called work.

Well, there's not much more to tell… Isn't this satin lovely? You look happy, Anna. You are so beautiful, darling. I am so proud of you. When you asked for this story as a wedding present you did not expect such a long one, did you? Well, there is a little more I must add. I'll tell you what happened this morning, and then we will be done…

Arrangements for your wedding have necessitated a number of meetings between James and me, Anna. Last week, I saw him speaking to my mother at the wedding rehearsal. He looked across at me several times, shaking his head once or twice. My heart sank. I knew my mother was saying things she shouldn't. Later, just before we left the church, he seemed to want to say something to me, but held back because Riaan came up to offer his arm to me as we walked down the stairs.

Well, I thought, that's how it always is, and always going to be. Just like it's always been. And I don't care, James McKelvey. I just don't care. I tucked Riaan's arm under my own, with a face like a sulky adolescent, causing both men, one at either side of me, to look at puzzled. However, after Riaan had dropped me off at Heritage, I was defeated by the most overwhelming sense of loneliness I had ever experienced. Soon your room would be silent and empty. You laughter would vanish. I would see you at weddings and funerals, at dinners and teas. There would be not a soul left between my waiting and me.

It was time I asked Riaan to move in. I could try to make him happy. It would give me something to do. What could be the harm in that? What harm could there be in trying to make him happy after all he had done for me?

"Can I get you something before you will be retiring, Miss Joss?" Krivahnen said gently. I sat up quickly and took my hands from my eyes.

"Oh… No, Krivahnen, no. Thanks."

Krivahnen hovered next to the chair, busying himself arranging the tray beside me. There was a long silence.

"Miss Joss," he said. "You are appearing to me that you are not in full enjoyment of your happiness. May I not be serving you a soothing evening beverage for this troubled mood that is upon you? A little spiced tea, perhaps?" I promptly burst into tears. Krivahnen looked gravely at me and removed a spotless hanky from his pocket. I took it gratefully.

"I'm such a fool, Krivahnen? I'm sitting here pining for James, just as I always do. All my life I've sat here and waited for James. Waited and waited for him to tell me he cares about me. Why can't I develop some sense of propriety... some dignity..."

Krivahnen held a finger up, his face clearing. I blew my nose and smiled ruefully at him through my tears. His face was compassionate, patient and open.

"I have something here you would surely be considering the use of, Miss Joss. Be waiting one brief moment." He returned with a pen and a sheet of paper.

"It is time," he said, "to take the horns of fate in your hand. I shall wait outside until you have finished the composing of this letter, and in the morning it shall be delivered to sir by my hand." He placed the writing instruments on the table beside me. "I remain until the task is done," he continued insistently. "I have no longer been having the desire to be seeing you thus, Miss Joss. Write the letter. You will be forgiving me for saying to you that it is time to be ceasing such stupidities. It is time for a heart full of courage and for forthright words." I put my hand out and he grasped it between his own slender fingers.

I picked up the pen and wrote the following letter:

278

James

I love you. I have always. And I always will. I have loved you for as long as I've been conscious of being able to love you. Forgive me if I cause you further pain for saying so, but I cannot be without you any longer.

James, please understand. I have tried so hard to do without you, knowing how you feel. I cannot do without you. Please come to me.

Joss

No sooner had Krivahnen left than I began to regret such foolishness. Once again I was putting James under the pressure of my unrequited feeling. I was good at doing that. How would I face him now? But face him I would have to. Your wedding was just a day or two away. We would have to play our appointed roles side by side knowing what I had so unguardedly written. How uncomfortable it was going to be. How could I have been so bold, so presumptuous, so devoid of consideration for him?

When he did not answer immediately I knew with a further desperate sinking that I had finally overstepped the last goodwill of our long acquaintance. Then my heart felt stripped of emotion. All my life, the cost of loving James had stripped my heart bare. It was an anguish I could no longer survive

But... I got a reply this morning, Anna. His letter came this morning. Krivahnen put it on the tray but I left it unopened for an hour. I stared resolutely across the lawns. Letter change lives. It lifted slightly as the wind slid across it. It had to be opened. The ivory letter opener lay beside it, placed there with Krivahnen's usual meticulous care. I stood up, picked up my riding crop and began to pace across the shafts of light that pierced the dense bougainvillea. Then flicking the crop against the top of my boot, I resolved to open the envelope.

Oh James, I thought, what now, what now?

Two sheets of paper rustled between my fingers. I wanted to *un*write words, unsay things, draw them back again...so I should not have to read this... but the reply was on this paper. It needed to be read.

I had a visit from your mother, Titch, just before your letter arrived yesterday, I perused from his spidery scrawl. *She told me everything, Joss.*
I also want to say I received a letter from Riaan that arrived some days before yours. This letter helped me understand a number of issues between you and me. Why did you not tell me about Anna, Joss. I would have been a better support to you, if you had. I put his letter down for a moment and pushed the lamenting of my heart aside. *There is much for is to discuss, Joss, much, and we will do so. James.*

I picked up the second folded sheet from the tray where it had fallen. It was a letter from Riaan to James!

December 1999

James

Here is some information I wish to give you to make things easier for Joss. I have loved Joss for much longer than you think. Anna is my daughter, not Peter's as everyone thinks. I had an affair with Joss just before Peter died and Anna was the precious result. But Joss does not love me. However long and hard I have denied it these twenty years, Joss turned to me at that time from loneliness and despair, not, by any means, because she was in love with me.

In respect for Joss's wishes, and in deference to Peter's memory, I have kept quiet all this time. I only found out about Anna when she was fifteen and she found out about me a year or two later.

To tell you of this is hard for me, but even harder for me is knowing how Joss suffers. So I must tell you a few things. We are the closest of friends. Joss has never lied to me or led me on. She has told me that she cannot marry me. My status as Joss's "partner" has come about by default, not by love. I have everything to give her, including my heart, man, but she will never be mine.

It turns out that Joss loves you and she believes she will never love anyone else. You are lucky, Boet. I know you have had your own rough road but I would give everything to be in your shoes. Please consider her feelings, James. She is worth a great deal to us both.

Riaan Berkhout

My tears fell unheeded until a sudden sound caused me to look up. I rose, my hand at my throat. James walked across the veranda. "Look, Titch, look here…" he said proffering his hand. In it lay a crystal frog, perfect in every detail. "It's for the other one. It belongs to the other one." I found my cheek against his shoulder, his hand at my back, and the long lean lines of him welding into me.

And that is how Milly found me on the

veranda this morning drinking in his skin, his breath, his mouth, murmuring with the voices and songs welling up from my ecstatic, vaulting heart.

"Well now, well now, this is something," she said. "Another McKelvey-Whitney wedding coming up. Oh my dears... how wonderful, how very wonderful!"

EPILOGUE

It seems that history itself has passed through the arches of this building. An air of mounted soldiers and well-bred horses has never left it, although more than a century has passed since its sables and billets became halls and reception rooms. The building lies on the beach a stone's throw from Mount Edgecombe. It is, usually, the province of men, and old ones at that. Retired and rich, they gather at the Country Club in small mutually supportive groups, totter from Merc's and BM's to read foreign newspapers and eat carefully prepared curries, and then fall asleep dyspeptically in overstuffed leather chairs. However, on this particular late afternoon, the gentlemen regulars have been relegated to the smoking room, harrumphing and tut-tutting, or have been sent home to lonely single gentlemen's quarters until Sunday breakfast, all because there is a wedding on

The wedding hall, overlooking the greenest golf course in Natal, is ideal for its purpose, delicate apricot flowers on the palest orange linen reflect in small glasses of crystal and huge polished windows compete with the settling sun for their share of dusk.

Expectant of being well fed and well watered, guests await the bride, getting to their feet when she arrives, clapping and smiling. She is, like the flowers in her hand, perfect and beautiful. Beside her, the new young husband, groomed and polished stands the groom, with her lace and satin dress draped across his feet.

Behind them, two couples. Edward McKelvey, grandfather of the groom, leans toward Hanna McKelvey, grandmother of the bride. Their hands are clasped and he listens intently as she speaks amid the applause of the assembled company. This family, now doubly tied by recent wedding ceremonies, moves towards the table of honour. Behind them, a little apart, somewhat uncertain, the bride's mother, Joss Whitney, and next to her, James McKelvey, father of the groom.

The party is settled at the table, anxiously overseen by an elderly Indian gentleman. He has been present at every wedding party since the marriage of Kiernan Whitney to the bride's grandmother five decades ago. He is particular to make Joss Whitney, mother of the bride and of whom he is most fond, comfortable at the groom's right. After the family is seated, much to the surprise of some guests who know the family well, shows Riaan Berkhout, to the left of the bride. Then he settles elderly Aunt Milly at Edward's side and directs Uncle Beau's tottering steps towards Hanna, where he subsides, whisky in hand. He returns to his place behind Anna and Dean and waits with composure and happiness.

There is a sense of continuity and joy at this table which many of the guests are already noticing as being exceptional. Glasses clink, friends hail one another, and there are only momentary gaps for speeches in the laughter and ribald remarks and the increasingly diffuse noise of people enjoying themselves. The young groom gets to his feet. He appeals for silence.

"It is usual," he says, "for the groom to thank the parents of the bride. And I would like to do that." He pauses to allow a few rude comments by his rowdy young friend, and then continues. "On this day I thank Johanna Whitney, Joss, for my lovely wife, Anna." The people clap loudly. "And then I would like to thank Anna's father, Riaan, for letting me have her." There is a stir in the assembled room. Has the young man made a slip of the tongue in his nervousness? However, he continues unabated. "Also, at this point, I should like to remember my mother, Kerry McKelvey." There is a break in his voice as he says her name. "She would have been so proud to be here today. Anna's mom was her best friend, you know." Women are starting to weep and men to clear their throats. "And I want to thank my dad, James McKelvey. Dad, I am so proud to bear this name. If I ever become half the man you are, I will have done my life, and Anna, well. You're the best, Dad." James McKelvey looks down hard at the floor, and then looks full in his son's face and smiles.

The guests do not fail to see Joss Whitney's intense involvement in this exchange. Indeed, they are watching Joss and James, and Riaan, most carefully.

The boy, for so he seems then, turns to his new wife, his eyes ablaze. He reaches for her hand and says steadily, "Anna, darling, I am so glad you are mine." Aunt Millicent sobs audibly. Then, with Anna at his side, Dean McKelvey holds out his hand to Joss. "Come, Dad," he says holding out his other hand. The guests sit up, taking in this turn of events with more than fascinated interest. Joss and James get to their feet. "It is usual, also, that the bride and groom dance the first waltz on these occasions. But Anna... my wife..." He pauses and smiles. "My wife has just told me something I think you all should know. As a result I think it is fitting that my dad and Anna's mom get out on the floor." There is another stirring in the crowd, a murmur of surprise and excitement, a smattering of "I knew it! I knew it!" and a few calls of "And about time too!"

James takes Joss by the hand and they move to the center of the floor. The band strikes up the first bars of music. He sweeps her into his arms, she is looking into his face. They dance into the first sedate, beautiful steps of the waltz, their feet skimming the floor, but any one can see they are not there, they are dancing in the bronze skies of Mount Edgecombe, lost in splendour and light. The guests begin to clap and catcall. There is more than just a wedding here and they love it. Like all of us, they love the fulfillment of things.